Examinin
Cupboards

By
Stevie Turner

Copyright

ISBN: 978-1-5272-5337-7

Contents

Dedication

For all those whistle-blowers who are brave enough to step forward.

Description

Jill Hayes discovers that not all is as it seems in her new post as a college examinations administrator. When she turns whistle-blower and tries to report her findings to the authorities, she is horrified to discover that some people will stop at nothing to ensure her silence.

For readers' information, the actual exam question that sparked Jill's nightmare is a genuine one from 1999.

Chapter One

JILL HAYES
MAY 1999

"In effect, you've misled me on your CV." Sue Young's artificially enhanced blonde bob oscillated as she shook her head and gave an audible sigh. "Did you know that out of all the applicants you were taken on because you'd stated how you'd built an in-house database in your previous job?"

Jill Hayes detected a frisson of dislike flit in her direction from the exam manager's face before the woman continued her diatribe.

"And don't forget, what goes on here in Daxton College *stays* in the college. Not a word breathed to the press about exam results unless the principal agrees first."

The dislike had rapidly become mutual. Only two days of being an exams administrator had convinced Jill that her new manager was a genuine, first-class daughter of a bitch.

"I- It was a slip of the pen." Jill faltered. "I meant I had built *up* an in-house database of sponsors at the charity before it closed down. I didn't build the actual database; I'm not *that* technically minded. Sorry."

Jill noticed how Sue's lips had set into a straight line.

"You're supposed to stand in for me when I'm on holiday."

"Yes I know." Jill tried to stare the woman out. "Perhaps give me a chance to see what I can do?"

"Let's start with the Fideliter Board; the first lot of students will be down in half an hour to pay for their Health and Carers' exams taking place in July. I assume Marion has shown you how to use the till outside?"

The dressing-down in front of her colleague had made Jill feel about two inches tall. She nodded.

"Yes, once, but I might have to ask her again as I only *watched* yesterday."

With a *tut* of disapproval Sue turned on her heel and marched out of the room.

"Take no notice." Marion Riley shrugged as she watched Sue's retreating back. "She gets on *my* tits sometimes too."

"My stomach's in knots." Jill gave a mock shudder. "I can't seem to do anything right."

"If you have trouble with the till, just give me a shout." Marion's voice was reassuring. "Don't forget, they ring the bell when they arrive at the counter; you don't have to stand out there. Make sure they've filled in their entry forms properly."

"Thanks. I'll continue on with getting my head around putting last month's exam results on the database then, shall I?"

"Sure; ask if you've got a problem." Marion nodded. "Don't worry about Sue, she'll come round eventually."

Jill settled down but leapt up as soon as the bell rung, pleased that Sue had not returned from wherever she had gone. When she opened the office door she tried not to panic at the queue of students lining up at the counter.

"Okay." She smiled with a confidence she did not have. "Who's first?"

An oriental-looking young man held up his entry form.

"Me."

She checked the spidery writing on the front of the form.

"You haven't filled in your details properly." Jill waved the form about. "What's your name?"

"Dingxiang Zhang."

"Can you fill in the top line please?" She quickly returned the form to him together with a pen. "And that'll be eight pounds fifty."

The student handed over a twenty pound note and completed the form. Jill looked at the unfamiliar electric till with its myriad of buttons, and tried to remember the right ones to push in sequence in order to open the cash drawer. In front of her the queue fidgeted and shuffled about, while her heart sank further at the sight of Sue Young's overweight figure bearing down on the counter and sizing up the situation in one meaningful stare.

"Have you got a problem with the till? Did Marion not show you yesterday?"

Jill forced a smile.

"Yes, but only briefly. As I told you before, I just watched. Would you mind showing me again please?"

"I haven't got time." Sue looked at her watch. "I've got a meeting now. I've just come back to grab my diary. Try to remember what you've learned."

Jill was aware of the students' sudden interest in her plight, as behind her *the hated one* entered the office and reappeared a moment later clutching a folder before disappearing along the corridor. Desperate to rectify the situation and save face, she quickly punched in the key code to open the office door.

"Sorry Marion, please can you show me how to work the till again? There's a long queue out here. I'll write it down this time just to make sure."

To her relief her new friend stood up.

"Of course. Don't worry about asking, we all had to learn."

She could have hugged Marion as her colleague opened the till with ease.

"Just push this one and then *that* one after you've put the amount in and how much they've given you." Marion pressed a finger on the correct buttons. "Hi Dingxiang, we'll be with you in a minute."

Jill was too flustered to even begin to work out how much change to give the student, and was relieved to see it pop up on the display.

"Thanks Marion, I think I'll be okay now."

She handed out eleven pounds fifty pence change and placed the first completed application form into a wire basket on the counter. Twenty minutes later she had a pile of forms, a diminished line of students, and a fair to middling working knowledge of the till.

Chapter Two

Jill heaped some more mashed potato onto her teenage son's plate, and then added vegetables and a chicken pie, musing on how, no matter where he was in the house or garden, Jordan always seemed to know when dinner was being served. True to form, he appeared just as the sound of two loaded plates hit the table.

"I'm starving."

"You're *always* starving." Jill sat down and sprinkled some salt on her pie. "How'd it go at school today?"

"More revising for the GCSE's. Boring! How's your new job?" He picked up a forkful of potato and put it into his mouth.

Jill grimaced.

"The manager's got it in for me I think."

"Already?" Jordan looked up. "You've only been there two days!"

"I put on my CV that I'd built up a database at the charity offices, and I think she took it that I'd built a programme for a database from scratch."

"There's a bit of a difference!" Jordan laughed and chewed on a carrot.

"Well what do I know?" Jill sighed. "Now I can't do a thing right."

Jordan took a mobile phone out of his pocket.

"Dad sent me a text. We're going to Highbury on Saturday to see Arsenal play."

"It's not his weekend is it?" Jill dug her knife a little too forcefully into a piece of pie. "You're supposed to be revising."

Jordan shovelled more food into his mouth.

"I can do that when I get back. I know it all anyway."

"Of course you do." Jill laughed. "You're sixteen, why wouldn't you?"

"It's just *easy*, that's all."

She loved the bones of him. He had his father's mathematical brain but her own physical traits; dark auburn hair, a high forehead, and hazel eyes.

"Well, bully for you. I hope washing up's easy too, because it's your turn tonight."

"Oh, Mum…" Jordan chewed and heaved a sigh.

The nervousness started as soon as she parked the car and started walking up the steps towards Daxton College's main concourse. She recognised some of the students hanging about outside from her debacle at the cash till the day before, and kept her head lowered until she was halfway down the main corridor towards the Exams office. As she stabbed in the key code, she could see a shadowy figure through a small frosted glass pane in the top of the door. Screwing up her courage, she opened the door with a flourish and gave a smile to the only other occupant in the room who failed to look up, seemingly already absorbed in her work.

"Morning Sue."

There was a slight aroma of fried breakfast. Jill closed the door quietly and hung up her jacket awaiting a reply, which when it did arrive sounded somewhat unenthusiastic.

"Hi."

Jill walked to her desk stifling a sigh.

"Mind if I open a window? It's a bit stuffy in here."

Taking a lack of response as a green light to proceed, she pushed open the window, enjoying a fresh cool breeze replacing the unpleasant odour of eggs and bacon. As she switched on her computer, Jill was aware that Sue was staring at her.

"Have you ordered the Health and Carers' exam papers from Fideliter?"

"Yes." Jill nodded, pleased that for once she hadn't made a mistake.

Sue gave a faint *tut* of disapproval.

"Well, you should have waited. There'll be another group down today. I already told you that yesterday's students were only the first lot."

Her first heartsink moment of the day coincided with the door to the office opening. Jill noticed how the manager's response to Marion's arrival differed from her own.

"Hey Marion! How's it going? Sue smiled and raised an arm in greeting.

"Overslept." Marion hurried to her desk and sat down. "Sorry."

"No problem. You and Charlie still coming to the pub tonight?"

"Sure." Marion yawned. "Got to do something to mark your birthday haven't we?"

Jill listened to the conversation flowing easily between the two women, all the while wanting to be someplace else. However, she decided to grit her teeth and send her best smile in Sue's direction when there was a gap in the chatter.

"Happy birthday."

The manager's eyes fixed on her over the top of a pair of half-moon reading glasses.

"I'm leaving it to you today to get the timetable ready for June to put on the noticeboard outside. Have a look at the one that's already there for May, and then check on the computer system which exams are taking place in June. Marion will have the template. You can print out an A4 sheet and then enlarge it on the photocopier to A3 size."

"Right." Jill felt a rising panic. "I'll get to it right away."

It was a relief just to get out of the cloying atmosphere of the office even for a short while. Jill tried to take in the layout of the timetable amidst a growing sense of unease that she was in the wrong job, and that her basic computer skills were no match for the level of competence needed in the Exams office. As she returned to her seat she could only hope that Sue Young would be called out to another meeting quite soon.

She enjoyed a boost from Marion's sympathetic smile as she returned to her seat.

"I've already emailed you the template."

"Thanks Marion."

Jill refrained from looking in Sue's direction, and checked her email account. The attachment was there, *but what did she need to do with it?* She opened up the email and the template attachment, where May's exams were all set out neatly with times, dates, and room numbers. She had a sudden idea, and composed an email to Marion, all the while conscious of Sue's brooding presence at the desk opposite.

'Hi Marion, thanks for the template. Sorry to ask, but what do I have to do with it?'

Quick as a flash, the reply popped up in her inbox.

'Save it as 'Exams Template' to your desktop, and then do a 'File and Save As' and name it June 1999. Then you can delete all May's exams and put June's in. Make a new folder and put the new file in there, as you'll have to do plenty more of them.'

After thanking her new friend, Jill still had no idea of how to proceed. She felt like crying. The difference between a data input clerk and an exams administrator seemed to be as wide as the ocean as far as computer literacy was concerned. *The job was beyond her capabilities.*

"Are you okay?"

She could feel Sue's eyes staring at her, and decided to come clean rather than bother Marion again.

"I'm just trying to work out how to save the timetable template to my desktop."

Sue Young stood up and to Jill's horror walked over towards her and peered at her monitor. The aroma of fried bacon assailed her nostrils.

"What computer work *did* you actually do in your previous job?"

"Building up a list of people who donated to the charity." Jill had the start of now familiar butterflies in her stomach at the sound of Sue's voice. "I added their names and addresses to an in-house database, but I answered the phone mostly and took messages for the managers."

She heard an exaggerated and forceful exhalation of breath behind her.

"Open the attachment. Right click on it, and click the option *save*, then right click again, and click *save as*. Give the file a new name. Marion, could you go to Reception and pick up the post please?"

Jill wanted the earth to swallow her up, and knew what was coming as soon as Marion had left the office.

"Have you saved files to a folder before?"

"No." Jill shook her head. "I don't think so."

"Remember, you are on a three-month trial period here, and you have a lot to learn. At the moment I can't see you being able to stand in for me if I'm on holiday. As you know, Marion is only part-time." Sue gave another sigh. "On your desktop you can right-click and open up a new folder to put your timetable in."

"I'm so sorry." Jill felt like crying. "I'll do my best to pick it all up."

"Work on the timetable this morning, and then this afternoon there'll be some scripts to send to the examiners for marking."

Right at that moment, Jill wished her boss had given her the option to go home. She would have been out of the office as quick as a rat down a greasy pole.

Chapter Three

On her return from lunch Jill noticed that a large cardboard box had appeared on her desk. She looked up questioningly at Sue, who had just locked the cupboard containing boxes of unopened exam papers and returned scripts from students.

"Those are the completed scripts for the Leisure & Excursions' diploma. You need to check each one off against the names on the computer list, and make sure each script has the student's name at the top. Scripts without a name will need to be returned to the department for identification. I asked Marion to email you the list before she went home. The examiner's name to send them to is at the bottom of the list. Have you got it?"

Conscious of the manager's eyes upon her, Jill checked her inbox.

"Yes, I'll print out the list and check them all off."

An oppressive silence pervaded the room. Jill picked up the first script, which was written in a child-like hand and contained many spelling mistakes, grammatical howlers, and smudges.

She could not help but notice the first question on the exam paper after she had checked for the student's name:

'For one mark, name the four countries that make up the United Kingdom.'

She had to read the question once more to make sure she had read it right. Just for good measure she read the next question on the paper:

'For one mark, name England's capital city.'

She looked up at Sue, perplexed.

"How old are these students?"

Her boss regarded her suspiciously over the top of her reading glasses.

"Usually sixteen to nineteen. Why?"

"Well, these questions surely are aimed at kids who are around ten years old? I mean, the second one wants them to name England's capital."

Sue shrugged and carried on typing.

"It's not for us to discuss set questions from exam boards."

"But they're too easy!" Jill exclaimed, waving the script in the air. "Now I know why I'm always reading about the students' high grades in the local paper! And the spelling on this one is atrocious. Do they get marks knocked off for bad presentation like we did in the days of O levels?"

"Not usually, but again, it's not for us to question why. Don't forget your confidentiality clause; *what goes on in college stays in college.*"

Sue's voice carried enough authority for Jill to realise that she had better not push her luck any further. She carried on checking through the rest of the scripts in the box, which were all poorly presented and full of errors. At the end of the afternoon she gathered up the scripts into a large envelope, wrote the examiner's address on the front, and left it at Reception for posting. She walked to her car somewhat dispirited and unable to understand why young people approaching twenty years of age would be set such undemanding exam questions.

"What's for dinner, Mum?"

Jill opened the oven door and rolled her eyes to the heavens at her son's insatiable appetite.

"Baked cod, oven chips and peas."

"Lovely." Jordan plonked himself down at the kitchen table. "Guess what?"

Jill took a container of cooked peas out of the microwave.

"What?"

"I got one hundred percent for my mock science exam."

"Wow!" Jill turned around to face her son. "That's great!"

"Yeah, but the questions were really easy."

A warning bell sounded in her head on hearing her son's words. As nonchalantly as possible, Jill posed a question whilst dishing up.

"What sort of questions did you get asked then?"

"Oh… stupid ones like give an example of a reptile and a rodent, and one even asked what animals can be found in a zoo!"

Jordan laughed as he squirted tomato sauce onto his plate. Jill sat down opposite her son and picked up her knife and fork.

"So I assume all your friends had high marks too?"

"Course." Jordan nodded and ate a chip. "Who wouldn't?"

"Do you know the name of the exam board by any chance?"

Jordan chewed thoughtfully.

"Fideliter I think."

"Have you filled in that form I gave you for the apprenticeship at CoolingAir Limited?"

"Not yet. I was thinking of going to your college for a couple of years."

"CoolingAir will send you to the college for day release, teach you a trade, and pay you a wage at the same time. You won't get paid if you're a full-time student."

"Oh." Jordan looked up. "I didn't realise that."

"Aha!" Jill waggled a finger at him. "You haven't even read the info I put in your room, have you?"

"I'll do it after dinner."

"Make sure you do, otherwise somebody else might get there first."

"Dad and Yvonne want to take me to Crete for a week when school finishes."

Jill poured herself out a glass of water.

"That's fine. How are you getting on with Yvonne now?"

"Better than before, but I still don't think she likes me much." Jordan grimaced. "Dad said I had to try harder."

Jill nodded.

"You've had a lot of change to deal with. *I've* had trouble getting used to it all too, but we'll get there, you and me."

She flashed her son a sympathetic smile, and was rewarded by a nine stone whirling dervish running around the table to give her a hug before sitting back down again to wait for dessert.

Chapter Four

Feeling more relaxed while her boss was at a meeting, Jill picked up the first General Studies script and checked the student's name against her printed list. Previously being unaware of what the subject actually entailed, she turned over to the first question with interest.

'What would be kept in a kitchen cupboard?'

The student had answered the question in detail, with large child-like writing listing various tinned foodstuffs and packets of rice, together with jars of jams and pickles. Jill shook her head in disbelief, held up the script, and turned towards Marion.

"A six year old could answer this one."

"Probably." Marion nodded. "Why d'you think the college has such good exam results every year?"

"They're asking what would be kept in a kitchen cupboard!"

Marion laughed.

"Yep, that's about the level I'd expect."

"Why does nobody report Fideliter to the inspectors?" Jill sighed and scrutinised the script again. "This is hardly in the students' best interests."

"There are inspectors, although I've never seen one here. It's all about league tables, money and funding as usual." Marion shrugged. "Everything comes down to money in the end. Students have to take a back seat in this place."

Jill picked up the next script.

"It's a bloody scandal! We'll have generations of uneducated young people! The public need to know what their money's being spent on."

"I wouldn't if I were you." Marion whispered conspiratorially. "Just do your job and go home at the end of the day like I do. They've gagged us in the confidentiality clause, don't forget. Be like me, and say nothing to nobody."

Jill imagined her son's future excitement at being offered a day release course, and felt a wave of boiling anger wash over her. She could not say anything that might disillusion him; she would have to work alone. She checked on the name of the exam board for aspiring electricians, and to her great relief discovered that Fideliter were not setting the questions.

With Jordan out at his youth club, Jill sat down to compose a letter to the local rag, The Daxton Standard.

Dear Sir / Madam,

I have to send this letter anonymously, otherwise I might lose my job. Please publish this letter in next week's paper. I work at Daxton College, and have discovered that the students, usually aged 16 – 19, are being asked very simple exam questions that would not tax a 10 year old. This of course makes for excellent results at the end of the college year as everybody passes, which therefore incurs increased government funding and a higher ranking for the college in the league tables.

One of the questions on the General Studies Diploma examination paper asked the students to name things that would be kept in a kitchen cupboard! Keep in mind that these young people are mostly 16 – 19 years of age. It's a national scandal! Fideliter exam board serves all schools and colleges in the UK – something needs to be done about this.'

She looked through the previous week's newspaper to find the editor's contact details, addressed an envelope, and shoved the letter through the post box with more force than was necessary.

She looked surreptitiously under her cuff at the Rolex watch which Dan had given her all those years ago for her 30th birthday; she could hardly wait for the working day to finish. After taking a pile of scripts to the receptionist for posting, Jill stopped by the college shop to buy the latest edition of the Daxton Standard, and then walked down the main stairs towards the car park. In the privacy of her car she perused 'Letters to the

Editor', but could find no evidence that her own letter had been published. Perplexed, she picked up her mobile phone and dialled the number given just inside the front page. A clipped voice sounded in her ear.

"Daxton Standard."

"Could I speak to the editor please?" Jill's heart began to race.

"Who shall I say is calling?"

Jill wracked her brain for a suitable name.

"Miss Jordan."

"I'll put you through."

Jill heard a pleasant male voice at the other end of the line.

"Good afternoon. This is the editor. Can I help you?"

"Yes please." Jill managed to stop herself from talking too fast. "It was I who wrote to you about what's going on at Daxton College. Did you get my letter?"

"Ah, yes..." The voice trailed off. "Er... unfortunately we could not print it."

Jill could not keep the indignation out of her voice.

"Why not?"

"The letter is anonymous. You would need to give us your name and address for verification."

"I can't do that. I'm a single parent who needs the job, and there's a confidentiality clause on my contract."

"Well then...I'm afraid we cannot help you this time."

Inwardly raging, Jill stabbed at a button to end the call. As she started up the car's engine and drove away a little faster than usual, another idea came to her. She had no doubt that this one would work:

She would smuggle out one of the unused Health & Carers' exam papers when nobody was about, and send it with a letter to one of the national tabloids!

Chapter Five

"Please can you print out some labels for the spines of these new folders?"

She knew very well that Sue was hoping to catch her out. Jill decided to come clean straight away.

"I've never done labels before. Would Marion have a template by any chance?"

The expected sigh was not long in arriving.

"I'll email it to you. Marion won't be back until tomorrow now."

Right click, save as, and then save as 'Label' to the desktop. Jill was learning, but it would seem not as quickly as a certain person would have liked.

"How do you think your first month has gone?"

She looked up from her monitor and across at the woman she had come to loathe and detest.

"Awful. It seems I cannot please you no matter how hard I try."

There was an awkward silence before Sue cleared her throat.

"Oh."

Jill played on the manager's momentary embarrassment.

"I find you unapproachable and unsympathetic. I only have basic computer skills, which is why I made that mistake on my CV. My idea of building up a database and yours are obviously poles apart. I'm trying to learn, but you're not making it easy. My stomach is in knots the minute I walk through the door every morning."

She stared for as long as she could at Sue's brown eyes, which regarded her with steely determination her over the top of a pair of reading glasses.

"I realise now that the mistake was not intentional. However, your level of I.T competence is far below what is needed as an exams administrator. Unless there is a distinct improvement in your computer skills, then I'm afraid we will dispense with your services after the three month trial period ends."

Ashamed at her shortcomings, all Jill wanted to do was burst into tears and run out the door; never before had any of her past employers ever complained about her work. After a few deep breaths the shame turned to anger, and the anger spurred her on to clear the air once and for all.

"To be honest I don't want to stay on after three months, but take it from me that in the meantime I'll do my best to learn the skills I'm lacking. At the end of August though, I'm out of here. As for these so-called exams, they're farcical; a six year old could answer most of these questions with no trouble at all."

She detected a momentary expression of relief pass over the older woman's features. Jill reluctantly turned her gaze back to the computer screen and waited for the response.

"As I've said before, it's not for us to comment on Fideliter's set questions. I'm sorry you feel I am unapproachable. We've obviously both got off on the wrong foot. I'll help you as much as I can, and perhaps in a few weeks you can start looking online for vacancies at the college which might be more suitable for you."

Jill was unsettled by Sue's change in demeanour, but felt surprisingly glad that all their problems were now out in the open.

The letter on the mat bore a London postmark. Jill picked it up and tore open the envelope. A Fleet Street address was the first thing she noticed:

'Dear Mrs Hayes,

Thank you for your letter and the enclosed copy of the Health & Carers' exam paper from Fideliter. We understand your concerns, but due to the sensitive nature of the letter's contents we are unable to publish it. I hope that you understand.

Yours sincerely,

D. R Oldenshaw (Editor, London Borough Standard)'

What to do next? More than ever Jill was convinced a conspiracy of silence existed. She had a sudden futuristic and catastrophic image of millions of uneducated and unemployable teenagers with handfuls of A* exam certificates being unwittingly manipulated through *opium-for-the-masses* government-sponsored daytime TV propaganda.

She plonked herself down on the bottom stair and stared blankly at the letter, unaware that Jordan had come out of his room on hearing her return from work.

"You okay Mum?"

Jill came out of her trance, stood up, and switched her gaze to the upstairs landing, where Jordan's head hung over the bannister.

"I've had a bit of a disappointment, but I'll find another way around it."

Two young legs clad in fashionable jeans bounded down to greet her.

"What's up?"

She gave her son a quick hug.

"Oh…I've found out something at college that isn't good. But hey, tell me about your day first while I put the kettle on."

"Had my English exam, which was really easy, and then I cycled home. Couldn't wait to get out of there. Oh… and I've just filled in that form you wanted me to do for the apprenticeship."

"Great." Jill smiled at him and then followed behind him to the kitchen. "Can you remember any of your exam questions today?"

Jordan shrugged.

"What's a noun …what's an adjective…stuff we did in primary school. When's dinner?"

"About an hour. Have an apple or banana while you're waiting."

She switched on the kettle while Jordan rooted around in the fridge, emerging triumphant clutching a sausage roll.

"What's up at college then?"

"That's part of your lunch tomorrow." She shook her head. "Put it back and take an apple. Like you, I've found out the exam questions are too easy."

"Great!" Jordan reluctantly returned the sausage roll. "I'll pass with no sweat then!"

"But what good will it do you in the big wide world? Anyway, yours would be a different exam board." Jill sighed and made herself a cup of tea. "Do you know what one of the questions was in the Health & Carers' exams?"

"No, what?" Jordan took a huge bite of a Granny Smith.

"It asked you to write down what you would keep in a kitchen cupboard!"

"Blimey, that's bad. I agree." Jordan nodded.

Jill added a spoonful of sugar to her tea and gave Jordan the letter she had just received.

"I've written to the local paper and a national one. As you can see, they don't want to print anything, as it's obviously too controversial. I've decided I'm going to try and contact our Member of Parliament and see what he says."

Jordan gave a low whistle as he read.

"Why don't you write online in Open Diary? I can show you how if you like. You can write what you want to there. It'll be your diary, and nobody can stop you. You'd better use a pen name though, if you do."

Jill switched on the oven and took a pre-prepared casserole out of the fridge.

"I might take you up on that. I'll see what the MP has to say first. I'll send a copy of the exam paper as proof. Anyway…let me have that form you've just completed and I'll send it off to CoolingAir before it gets lost in the depths of your room."

Chapter Six

She decided not to wait for the inevitable dismissal. Jill leafed through the Daxton Standard, skipping over any positions which needed a modicum of computer experience. She sighed with the realisation that computers were gradually becoming the norm in any workplace, and that she must either struggle to learn a skill she was not really interested in, or accept lower paid jobs such as stacking shelves in supermarkets, frying burgers in fast food joints, or cleaning hotel rooms. Nothing she could see in the newspaper particularly appealed, and she was just about to give up when an advert right down at the bottom of the page caught her eye.

'Companion and daily housekeeper needed Monday – Friday for disabled lady. Cleaning, shopping, and cooking. No personal care. £5 per hour. Phone Ms Sally Davidge.'

Here was something she could do! Jill quickly dialled the telephone number given, and a nicely modulated voice came down the line.

"Hello?"

"Ms Davidge?"

"Yes."

"I'm Jill Hayes, I saw your advert in the newspaper."

"Ah, so you'd like to come for an interview?"

"Yes please."

Jill liked the sound of Sally Davidge's voice. She jotted down the address, which she noted was on the rather upmarket Charter estate, and agreed a time and date to attend. She replaced the receiver feeling somewhat uplifted with the sure and certain knowledge that herself and Ms Davidge would soon become firm friends.

"You're invigilating this afternoon for the Business Diploma Level One, so you'll need to get the exam papers out of the cupboard. You'll have the list of candidates from when you processed the entry forms. Get them to leave their bags and mobile phones with you at the front. All they're allowed to take with them to the desk is a clear pencil case."

Sue's tone was straightforward and without emotion. Jill was relieved to be able to escape the office and the feeling of doom that always accompanied her manager's oppressive presence. She jumped up and tried not to show too much joy.

"Sure. Can I have the keys to the cupboard please? I'll get the papers ready."

"Have you got a list of candidates?"

"No." Jill sighed. "But I'll print it out *now*."

Once safely in the store cupboard out of sight, she stuck up a middle finger in Sue's direction, and then concentrated on finding the correct box of papers. Each box had a security seal, and she was mindful of not incurring Sue's wrath further by opening the wrong box and rendering the papers invalid. Jill carried the correct box out to the office, double checking and triple checking the label before she broke the seal, her heart hammering with nerves.

"I hope you've opened the right box."

Jill forced a smile in Sue's direction.

"Business Diploma Level One, just like you said."

"I shouldn't have to say. You should already know by looking at the timetable."

There was a brief silence whilst Jill controlled her anger.

"I'll take out thirty papers and go to the lecture hall."

"Please do."

She slammed the door on her way out, the action filling her with unbridled joy. The lecture hall was soothingly silent and empty, and Jill took advantage of ten minutes of peace. She flicked open one of the exam papers and shook her head at the first multiple choice question and choice of three answers.

'Who is higher up in a hotel's chain of command? 1, a receptionist, 2, a general manager, or 3, a chambermaid.'

She could see the students crowding around outside, and walked towards the main entrance, her heels making a tap-tapping noise on the hardwood floor.

"Come in. Please leave your bags and mobile phones by my desk at the front, take your pencil case, and find a seat."

When the students were settled, Jill, carrying a pile of exam papers, walked up and down the lines of desks.

"Please do not turn over the paper until the two o'clock chimes have ended. You will have two hours to finish the exam."

The heat of the afternoon hung heavy in the lecture hall as thirty students scribbled away. Jill, full of a heavy canteen lunch of chicken pasta bake, fought the urge to doze in her chair. To keep herself awake she sauntered between the rows of desks, noticing how quickly the students were working. At the end of the first hour all but one had finished. When the last student put down his pen and looked at her, Jill addressed the group.

"Hands up those of you who are finished."

A sea of hands rose in front of her. She looked up at the clock, which showed ten minutes past one.

"Have a quick look through your answers and then collect your things and go. I'll gather up the exam papers presently."

A student in the front row laughed.

"It was real easy, Miss."

Jill could only silently agree with him.

"Do come in Mrs Hayes, it's nice to meet you."

Jill followed Sally Davidge's wheelchair from the black and white tiled entrance hall down a wide passage into a large, airy front room furnished in a modern style, which in turn led via open sliding doors to a patio garden with hanging baskets full of colourful trailing plants.

"Call me Jill, if you'd rather."

"I'm Sally." Sally turned the wheelchair around expertly. "Take a seat and we can have a chat. There's some water on the table if you like, or I can make you a coffee?"

"Water is fine, thanks." Jill poured herself a glass. "You have a lovely house here."

"Thank you. As you can see, I'm wheelchair bound as I'm an amputee. I need somebody to help keep the house clean and do some shopping for me every day." Sally replied. "My current lady is emigrating to Australia in a few weeks."

"Sure; I'd have no trouble with that." Jill nodded. "I live locally, but I'd need to give a month's notice at the college where I've not long started work." She grimaced. "The job isn't going too well, as I found out too late that I'm not very computer literate."

"Oh dear." Sally laughed. "Well, you don't need to be Einstein to work here; but I will need to see some references. I'm looking for somebody who is reliable and trustworthy."

"I'm sure my current employer can vouch for that." Jill mentally crossed her fingers. "But you can ask the manager of the charity where I worked previously for a reference too. I stayed there for three years before it closed down."

"Yes, please let me have their phone number and we can take it from there. I like to phone for references rather than have them written down. Do you have any children Jill?"

"One sixteen-year-old son. I'm divorced, so it's just Jordan and me at home."

"I envy you being a mother." Sally sighed. "I was never given that opportunity in life, and well…it's too late now."

Jill found herself warming to her new potential employer. She looked about at the obvious opulence of the room which seemed somehow stark and barren without a plethora of family photographs in ill-matching frames, the like of which currently adorned her own living area.

"How long have you been in a wheelchair?"

"A few months, but I knew it was coming and so I could prepare for it." Sally shrugged. "Side-effect of diabetes nobody tells you about until they have to. I do own a prosthetic leg, but it doesn't fit like it's supposed to. I'm waiting for the NHS to build me a new one."

Jill tried to lighten the atmosphere.

"I could do with more than a new leg, probably a whole new body would be best."

Sally laughed.

"I'm going to like you, I know it. I've got your contact details. Thanks for the phone number of your previous employer. I'll give them a call, and then I'll be in touch."

"Thanks for seeing me today." Jill stood up. "I look forward to hearing from you."

Chapter Seven

"Hey, CoolingAir's asked me to attend for an interview!"

Jill looked up from her Saturday morning treat of reading a newspaper from cover to cover to the sight of an excited Jordan running towards her and waving a piece of paper about in the air.

"Great!" She stood up and gave him a hug. "When?"

"On Monday week at half past four. I've only got an English Lit exam that morning, so I'll cycle home after and wait. I'll text Dad and let him know."

"They might ask how your GCSE's are going."

Jordan waved away her fears with one hand and picked up his mobile phone with the other.

"All the questions are so easy, Mum. *And* the teachers seem to know what questions we'll get."

"Do they?" Jill looked at Jordan with interest. "How do they know?"

"Probably someone's slipped them the exam papers on the quiet for a backhander." Jordan laughed. "When we're in class revising they give us a list of questions to answer, and more often than not they're the same ones we get on the actual exam papers."

Jill thought of the college's locked cupboard and the boxes of exam papers with their unbroken security seals.

"Nobody, not even us in the department, are allowed to open the boxes of question papers until just before each exam."

"Well, all I can say is that *somebody's* opening them." Jordan's fingers flew over his phone's keypad with ease. "Unless all the teachers are clairvoyant or have x-ray vision."

Jill sighed with her son's new revelation, making her all the more determined to pass on her fears to the local MP. After Jordan had cycled off to fry burgers in Daxton's one and only fast food joint, Jill picked up a pen and piece of paper.

'Dear Mr. Latimer-Brown,

I am writing to you in desperation. I work at Daxton College, and I have found out that students are being set exam questions that would not tax a six-year-old, with the obvious intention of giving out a false impression to parents that the college obtains good exam results. I have enclosed a copy of one past exam paper from the Fideliter Exams Board as proof. Also, my 16-year-old son admits that his teachers are giving out prior knowledge of GCSE exam questions to the pupils in their revision lessons, no doubt to boost their place in the school league tables. I have contacted local and national newspapers who understand the problem but are unable to publish my letters, which are considered too controversial. Please can you help? Something is very wrong here, and nobody seems to want to do anything about it.

Yours sincerely,
Jill Hayes (Mrs.)'

Within a few of days of her interview with Sally Davidge, Jill found a message on her answerphone after returning from work.

'Hi Jill, it's Sally. I phoned your old employer at the charity and he was very complimentary about you. I'd like to offer you the post at five pounds per hour starting...shall we say...nine o'clock on the first of August? Do ring me back when you receive this.'

A wonderful wave of joy washed over her. Jill picked up the phone and dialled Sally's number.

"Hello?"

"Sally, it's Jill. Thanks for your message. Yes I'd love to take you up on it."

"Great!"

Jill imagined Sally's grinning face at the other end of the line. There was one question she had to ask.

"Did you speak to Sue Young at the college?"

"No. When you said you were having trouble there I didn't bother."

"Oh, okay." Jill breathed a sigh of relief. "Thanks. I'll give my notice in and see you on the first of August."

"I look forward to it." Sally's voice sounded upbeat. "Bye for now."

Jill replaced the receiver and ran up the stairs to her son's bedroom.

"Jordan, I've got the job!"

She knocked lightly to no reply. Peeping around the door she saw the room was empty. Puzzled, she quickly returned downstairs, grabbed her mobile phone from her bag, and dialled Jordan's number. His voicemail cut in asking her to leave a message.

"Jordan, it's Mum. Call me when you get this."

She went into the kitchen and opened up the freezer, taking out two steak and onion pies. As she did so she looked idly towards the back door, which was slightly ajar. It then registered in her brain that her son's bicycle was standing propped up against the back wall like it always was. She went outside, expecting to see Jordan sunbathing or tinkering about in the shed. However, nobody was about, but the unlocked back gate swung back and forth in a light summer breeze. She locked the gate and re-dialled Jordan's number.

"It's Mum again. Have you walked up the road to see Andy? I'll do some dinner for six o'clock. Bye."

She found the quietness of an empty house somewhat depressing. Jill turned the radio up loud and prepared some vegetables, realising that she would have to get used to Jordan's absences as he grew older and became more independent. She peeled a potato and thought back to her, Jordan and Dan and their secure little family unit before Yvonne's corrosive influence had blown it all apart.

On the dot of six o'clock she placed two steaming pies with vegetables and gravy on the table and sat down to eat. When she finished her meal, she covered Jordan's untouched food with a microwave plate, put the crockery in the dishwasher, and sauntered along the road to Brenda and Dave's house three doors down. After knocking on the door, she noticed that Brenda seemed surprised to see her. She smiled and looked past her neighbour into their hallway.

"Hi, is Jordan with you?"

"No." Brenda shook her head, puzzled. "Andy hasn't seen him at all this evening, and he can't get him on the phone."

A niggling worry began to circulate in her head. Jill made her exit, ran home, and picked up the phone, relieved to hear her ex-husband's voice.

"Dan, is Jordan with you?"

"No. Why do you ask?"

She heard Yvonne's voice in the background, but carried on regardless.

"He hasn't come home for dinner. His bike's in the garden, but he's not at Andy's."

"He's sixteen. Did you tell your mum where *you* were when you were sixteen? He's probably out with a girl somewhere. Don't fret; he'll be home when he's hungry."

She failed to be reassured by her ex-husband's words. Jill replaced the receiver and waited for Jordan to return home, filled with a nagging sense of unease.

Her son's dinner had cooled enough by 8 o'clock for her to cover it with cling film and put it in the fridge. She closed the fridge door just as the phone rang. She ran down the hallway and grabbed the receiver.

"Hello?"

"Jill Hayes?" A male voice came down the line. "Is that Jill Hayes?"

"Yes. Who's speaking?"

"This is Archie Latimer-Brown. You sent me a letter this week."

"Oh, yes." Jill had momentarily forgotten about her letter. "Can you help me?"

"Not really. You need to make a disclosure to Starfaire, the Exam Regulatory Board. The college will have the address somewhere I expect. Whistle-blowers are protected by law, so you won't lose your job."

"Thanks, but I'm going to give in my notice anyway."

Starfaire will investigate any claims you make. I'll send the exam paper back to you."

"Thank you."

She hung up and wondered for the umpteenth time where her son had got to.

Chapter Eight

Towards ten o'clock that night she heard a tapping on the front door. She opened the door to Jordan, who fell upon her, bloodied and bruised.

"Oh my God!" Jill sat her son down on the carpet and shut the front door to block out nosey neighbours. "Whatever's happened to you?"

Jordan regarded her through his right eye, which had not completely closed up.

"Don't know." He hissed; his pale face grimaced in pain. "I was dragged out of the back garden, had a sack put over my face, and then driven to somewhere quiet in a car. When they took the hood off, I saw two blokes wearing balaclavas. They attacked me and I was sick. We were in the middle of a forest, I think. I stayed lying on the ground until they put me back in the car and chucked me out just now.

"We need to get you to hospital." Jill tried to keep the panic out of her voice. "You've had a head injury."

"They said no hospital and no police. They threw my phone away. All they said was to tell you stop writing any more letters."

An ice-cold stab of fear passed through her body. Jill rammed home the deadlock on the front door and helped Jordan to his feet.

"Come and lie down on the settee. I'll bring some warm water and clean you up a bit."

"Who have you been writing to, Mum?" Jordan staggered into the front room and fell onto the sofa. "What have you said? Whatever it is, someone doesn't like it."

Her heart beat frantically in her chest as she returned from the kitchen and gently cleaned away dirt and debris from Jordan's wounds and applied some anti-bacterial ointment.

"It was all about the easy exam questions. I tried to get the newspapers interested, but they wouldn't print my letter."

"Ouch!" Jordan let out a howl of protest.

"Sorry." Jill winced. "Are you sure nothing's broken?"

"They knew what they were doing. Just enough force to frighten me off."

"They've certainly frightened *me*." Jill let out a long sigh.

"So, no more letters, Mum?" Jordan looked at her out of his one good eye. "Anyway, I like easy exam questions 'cos I'll get good grades then!"

She shook her head.

"The Fideliter exam board is obviously corrupt. Schools and colleges are using *their* exam questions because all the students pass, the league tables look good, and Fideliter earns more money through the students' fees."

Jordan leaned back in his seat.

"Does that mean I'm thick?"

"No, not at all." Jill gave her son a brief hug. "It means that you're not being taught properly. If only I could have sent you to a public school."

"With all those Ruperts and Tarquins? I'd have been bog-brushed on my first day!"

She allowed a faint smile to cross her lips.

"Sit there and recover. You really shouldn't have anything to eat for the moment, and *don't* go to sleep."

"I'm not sleepy." Jordan shook his head. "But I'm starving."

"Wait an hour or so. And then I'll warm your dinner up in the microwave."

"Cheers Mum." Jordan gave her a thin smile.

'It's a shame you're going." Marion gave Jill a brief hug. "We haven't had a chance to get to know each other properly."

Jill returned the hug with one eye on the door, dreading their manager's return from lunch.

"I think Sue will be glad to see the back of me, but there's one thing I must do before I go."

Marion looked at Jill with interest.

"Oh?"

"I need to find out the address of Starfaire. Do you know whereabouts in the office it is?"

"Sure." Marion nodded. "It's in the locked cupboard with the exam papers. Why d'you need it?"

Jill wasn't sure if her colleague was trustworthy enough, so decided not to come totally clean.

"I want to write to them about something."

Marion put on a cardigan and picked up her bag.

"Sue has the key, although she usually leaves it in the top drawer of her desk if she's out of the office. I'm off now, but I'll see you in the morning."

"Okay."

She had the location. Hopefully there would now be enough time to grab the key, nip into the cupboard, and find the address before her period of notice came to its natural end. *Heads needed to roll at Fideliter before they failed yet another generation of young people!*

Chapter Nine

The Daxton Standard had its centre pages dedicated to individual exam successes at the college. Jill could not bear to read the drivel spouted by the grinning principal, and screwed the newspaper up into a tight ball.

"Of course, it's another record year for passes, just as long as the students are given questions for six-year old's!"

She lobbed the paper at Jordan, who batted it away with one hand as he sent a text with the other.

"Leave it Mum. You've settled in with Sally now. Don't stir it all up again."

"Just look at his stupid face droning on about A star results. It makes me want to slap him! For all we know it could have been *him* who had you beaten up if the Daxton Standard showed him my letters."

"Who knows? But if you like I'll slap him for you when I start there in September on my electrician's course."

Jill stared at her son.

"How d'you know you're going to start there in September?"

Jordan put his phone down and took a piece of paper out of his pocket.

"Because of this." He folded it into a paper aeroplane and launched it at Jill. "Look what the postman brought me this morning."

She unfolded the letter and quickly scanned its contents.

"Oh, that's great news! You've got the apprenticeship at CoolingAid!"

"Yeah." Jordan shrugged. "I'm starting in a fortnight. Fifty-seven pounds sixty a month. I'll be rich!"

"All the time you're living *here* you will be. Have you told Dad?"

"I'll tell him next week when we're in Greece. Did you get me some new swimming trunks?"

"Yes, they're in your drawer; I already told you." She smiled at him. "Well done Jordie, well done."

She could see that her efforts were going some way to not only brightening up the house, but also to improving Sally Davidge's mood. Jill was aware her new employer looked forward to her daily visits, and after the fiasco of her college non-career, Jill had finally found contentment in something she was able to do well. Each day she got to know Sally a little better, and felt increasingly comfortable enough to share a little of herself.

"Are you divorced like me?" Jill picked up and carefully dusted a Capodimonte porcelain figurine.

"Yeah." Sally rolled her eyes towards the ceiling. "He sure took off when he found out my diabetes was progressing."

"Sounds like you're well rid of him." Jill placed the figure back where she found it. "My man had the hots for the wonderful Yvonne."

"All men are bastards, aren't they?" Sally replied with more than a trace of bitterness.

"Well, our two were for starters." Jill laughed as she polished the coffee table. "Want a cup of tea?"

"I can do that myself as you know, but as you're offering…" Sally nodded. "That will be great. No sugar though. Make one for yourself too."

Jill busied herself in Sally's now familiar kitchen, returning to the front room to see that Sally had wheeled herself out onto the patio.

"Here you are." Jill placed a steaming cup on Sally's tray. "I'll get on with the vacuuming now, shall I?"

"Sit here for a bit and have a break with me."

Jill sipped her tea and enjoyed the bright, sunny morning.

"Where did you work before, Sally?"

Sally picked up her cup with both hands and took a tentative sip.

"I was a DI in the Daxton Police Force. Still am really, but I'm on extended sick leave until they can find me a desk job."

"Goodness!" Jill looked at Sally with undisguised surprise.

"Yeah, you wouldn't think so to look at me now, would you? I was born with Type One diabetes, so I haven't stuffed myself silly with junk food, but the disease takes its toll as you get older… reduced circulation, foot ulcers, eye problems, and …. well… you can see the rest."

Jill sensed the depression that her new friend was trying to keep hidden, but Sally's revelation had started her brain racing.

"Do you still keep in touch with your colleagues?"

"Sure. They invite me to the Christmas meal, although I always politely decline. They stopped the annual ball invitation after Mike left."

As Jill emptied her cup she wondered if Karma had sent her in Sally's direction. She stood up to resume work, but could not help blurting out the secret she had kept inside for months.

"I bet you and your colleagues would be interested in something I've found out."

"Oh?" Sally looked up at Jill with interest.

"My son was assaulted recently, and I think I know why. I wrote a letter to the Daxton Standard about what's going on at the college, but didn't put my name and address on it. They wouldn't print it. As you know, I used to work there, and I discovered the students were sitting exam questions that wouldn't tax kids over half their age. Then recently my son was dragged out of our back garden and beaten up, with the instruction to tell me to stop writing any more letters, and not to go to hospital or to the police."

"Serious stuff." Sally turned her wheelchair around to face Jill. "Have you got any evidence?"

"I managed to smuggle out an exam paper, which I've still got. I'd also written to the London Borough Standard, but the editor wouldn't print that either – too controversial apparently. I then wrote to Starfaire – the Exam Regulatory Board, but I haven't heard a word." Jill gave a rueful laugh. "Perhaps they're involved as well."

A silence followed, which was broken first by Sally.

"When you come tomorrow, bring the exam paper. I'll phone the right people and get the ball rolling for you but I won't mention your name. I'll ask my colleagues to have a bit of a sniff around and check out whether anyone from Starfaire is carrying out any investigations."

"Oh God – I'll be frightened to go home or let Jordan out of my sight!" Jill shook her head. "This is not something the powers-that-be want out in the open."

Sally nodded in agreement.

"Can he stay with his dad for a while?"

Jill sighed while imagining the logistics.

"I suppose so, but he likes the wonderful Yvonne even less than I do. It'll be nearer his place of work though, so it won't take so long for him to cycle."

"See how things work out." Sally replied. "If needs be the police can find you a safe house. For the moment they'll give you a special number to ring if you're worried. This needs investigating, especially now after your son was attacked."

"Thanks Sally. I'll get on with the vacuuming now."

"Mum, I really *don't* want to go and stay with Dad and Yvonne!"

Her heart went out to Jordan, but there was no other way around it.

"I know, but it's best while the police investigate who might have attacked you. We don't want a repeat performance."

"Yeah, but..."

"I've already spoken to Dad. He's picking your stuff up on Friday evening. At least it won't be as far to cycle to work."

She wanted to hug away the look of dismay on his face.

"She didn't want me there in Greece, let alone living in her house."

"It'll just be for a few weeks." She kept her voice bright. "Things might get a bit nasty."

"And who's going to look after *you*?" Jordan asked in a worried voice.

She shrugged away his fears.

"Your course will be a standard electrician's one and not through Fideliter, but there are many students at the college who *are* getting short-changed. They'll have diplomas coming out of their ears, but they're worthless. Any employer will have to send them on another course to give them a basic education, and all the while that...that *Principal* John Bream is being kept in a job and taking taxpayers' money. It's a scandal."

"Do you have to be so noble, Mum? Can't you just leave it? We can carry on as normal then."

Jill shook her head.

"Sorry love, but it could have been *you* taking one of those Mickey Mouse courses."

She blinked back tears at the sight of her son standing so resolute next to his father.

“Thanks for this, Dan. Sally told me yesterday that the investigation is now under way.”

“No probs.” Dan Hayes ruffled Jordan’s hair. “Call me when you get any news.”

“If they only find out who attacked Jordan I’ll be happy. The exam conspiracy thing is secondary as far as I’m concerned.”

“Bye Mum.” Jordan stepped forward and gave her a hug. “I wish you hadn’t started all this.”

She watched them walk down the path towards the car, her son’s last words ringing in her ears.

The house was too quiet without Jordan. She usually liked lying in bed a little bit longer on Sunday mornings, but agitated and unable to settle, she found herself vacuuming already-clean rooms at half past seven instead. Outside not even a bird chirruped in the humidity, and the effort of housework was making her sweat. After cleaning the entire house, she jumped in the shower and then checked her phone whilst she towelled herself dry.

‘Don’t forget, you can always call me if you’re worried.’

How about lonely? Or how about just downright bloody angry that you broke your marriage vows?

Jill deleted Dan's text, slammed her phone down on the side of the bath, closed her eyes, and counted to ten. When her breathing was regular, she went downstairs to the kitchen and sent a text to Jordan, not expecting a reply until around noon, his usual Sunday morning waking up time.

After grilling a comforting bacon sandwich, she decided to stride out into Daxton's local park before the four walls of her sitting room began to close in. Dressed in a white tee-shirt, trainers, cropped blue pedal-pushers, and the special watch that Dan had bought her and which she never took off, Jill walked to the end of the street and across the railway bridge to the park's entrance. No runners were about, just sleep-deprived parents with lively toddlers in the swing park over the far side. She stepped up her pace and began to power-walk along the jogging track. As she walked she checked the second hand on her watch to see whether she could beat her personal best time.

The air was thundery, oppressive. Jill felt beads of sweat itching on her back within minutes, but carried on increasing the pace. During her second lap she saw a dark Chelsea tractor-like car pull up by the park gates. A forty-something man wearing a tracksuit got out of the car and jogged in through the gates. On hearing his footsteps thudding close behind her, she moved over to one side of the path to let him pass. However, he jogged up close to her, slowed down, and Jill felt her arms being held in a firm grip.

"Don't fight."

She could not move her arms, but she could still scream. Jill opened her mouth and took a deep breath of something which to her had an essence reminiscent of a dentist's surgery. No sound seemed to come out although she tried in vain to make her voice carry over to the parents of the toddlers in the swing park. She remembered nothing more after that.

Chapter Ten

SALLY

Sally Davidge looked at the clock again and wondered where on earth her new friend could have got to. It was unlike Jill to be late. She picked up her mobile phone and dialled Jill's number, which went automatically to voicemail. She wheeled herself over to a side unit and opened a drawer. Inside she found just what she was looking for; the next of kin contact details that Jill had written down on her first day. She tapped in the number for Dan Hayes. A pleasantly deep voice answered her call.

"Hello?"

"Dan Hayes?"

"Yes. Who's calling please?"

Sally did not want to cause unnecessary alarm, and so tried to keep an even tone.

"This is Sally Davidge, Jill's employer. She gave your number as a contact. Do you know if she is ill? She hasn't turned up for work today."

There was a slight hesitation before she heard a reply.

"I haven't heard from her, but I've got a key. I'm at work at the moment, but I'll pop round and check at lunchtime."

"Thanks." Sally replied, with evident relief. "You've got my number now; I'll wait to hear from you."

She still had the back-up of the homecare agency. Sally dialled the number she knew off by heart and booked a carer for the day. Their hourly rate had increased somewhat since she had last needed to use them, and she fervently hoped that whatever Jill was suffering from, she very soon made a speedy recovery.

At three fifteen that afternoon her phone buzzed, waking Sally from a fitful doze.

"Hello?"

"Ms. Davidge, this is Dan Hayes. I went round to Jill's just now but she's not there. I looked all over the house. There's the remains of a bacon sandwich on the kitchen table, but the crusts are hard. It's strange that she hasn't washed the plate up, and I can't believe she ate that today. Her phone's in the kitchen too. Something doesn't feel right."

"Oh God." Sally tried to keep the panic out of her voice. "She was worried after Jordan was attacked. Not turning up here is quite out of character I think."

"Yes, you're right." Dan replied. "I knocked on the neighbours' doors as well, but nobody's seen her. Taking what happened to Jordan into consideration, I'm going to report her as missing. She would have phoned you if she was ill."

"I'll phone my old colleagues at the station and do the same." Sally sighed. "I just hope nothing's happened to her."

As soon as she had ended the call, Sally phoned another number that she knew like the back of her hand. A familiar voice came down the line.

"Rich, it's Sally. I've got an update for you on that exam conspiracy."

"What you got Sal?"

Richard Jones was all ears, she could tell.

"Jordan Hayes' mother Jill is missing. She works for me but didn't turn up this morning. Her husband's going to report her as a missing person. Have you found out anything?"

"Only a big wall of silence. Starfaire have denied ever receiving a letter. Fideliter are owned by a big publishing company, Accelerat, who provide all the textbooks and educational needs for the schools and colleges who take their exams. Seems that interviewing the MD of Accelerat is going to be the next step, if we can track him down."

Sally gave a rueful laugh.

"I expect he's tending to his offshore bank account."

"You're probably not far wrong."

Sally missed her new friend. She felt powerless to do anything practical to help find Jill, but was relieved to still be in touch with her colleagues at the station. In this way she could glean as much information as she could to pass on to Dan Hayes.

She wheeled herself over to her computer and switched it on, searching for *Accelerat*. Smiling at her were the self-satisfied features of one Linus Eden Ewing, Managing Director, below perfectly coiffed light brown shoulder length hair streaked with obvious bleached blond highlights. She gave a loud snort on discovering how Linus was aged 45 and resided in St. Helier, Jersey, with his wife and four children. The *'Contact Me'* page gave a P.O Box address on the Island.

Sally disliked the look of him on sight.

Chapter Eleven

DAN

"Why have you reported her missing? She might be staying with a boyfriend or something like that. It's none of your business!"

Dan Hayes sensed the usual irritation in Yvonne's voice which only seemed to appear at the mention of his ex-wife's name.

"Yes it *is* my business." He replied forcefully. "Jordan's been beaten up, and Jill's worried now that the police are involved. What's more, her phone's still on the kitchen table, and she usually takes it everywhere."

"I still say she's off somewhere with a lover." Yvonne sniffed.

Why should he mind even if she was? Dan however realised that actually, yes he *did* care. The thought of an unknown man sleeping with his ex-wife caused a sudden surge of anger to rise up from his core.

"Jordan would have told me if there was another man about."

"So the saintly Jill sits at home and knits for ever more?" Yvonne rolled her eyes. "Come on!"

With one fluid movement Dan rose from the settee and walked out of the room. He took the stairs two at a time to where his son sat morosely on his bed in the guest room.

"How was work?"

Jordan finished sending a text and shrugged.

"Okay. They're trying to build up my muscles. I've been sawing bits of wood all day. Any news about Mum?"

"Not yet." Dan shook his head. "Fancy coming out to try and find her?"

"Sure." Jordan jumped up with alacrity. "Where shall we start?"

Dan didn't have the foggiest idea.

"Probably best to begin at home. Let's go and have a search round and see what we can find."

The crust of bread had the beginnings of a mould spot. Dan picked up the plate and threw the crust in the bin.

"I'll do this bit of washing up first. It's obvious Mum hadn't meant to be out for long."

It felt like old times standing at the sink, when he would wash and Jill would wipe. Dan left the frying pan and dripping crockery on the draining board and went out into the back garden, closely followed by Jordan.

"The gate's still locked from the inside." Jordan slid back the bolt. "Nobody's been here."

Dan walked over to the open gate and looked up and down the side alley. Jordan slapped a hand to his forehead and took his phone out of his pocket.

"Dad, I've just remembered something."

"What?" Dan looked down over his son's shoulder at the display screen.

"Mum sent me a text on Sunday morning. I meant to read it, but I didn't wake up until one o'clock and then Yvonne said it was dinner time." Jordan peered intently at the screen. "She says she hopes I'm doing okay at work, and that she's going out for a walk but will phone me later."

Dan hid his annoyance and locked the gate.

"So where would Mum be most likely to go?"

"The park." Jordan shrugged. "Probably."

He noticed with some relief that the more recent photographs in the album just depicted his ex-wife and Jordan. Dan made a mental note to put Yvonne straight, and slid out a recent photo of Jill.

"Let's take this along to the park and see if anybody recognises Mum from Sunday."

A few bored-looking teenagers sat under a tree, passing around what looked to Dan like a bottle of cheap cider.

"Were you here on Sunday morning?" He held up the photo. "Did you see this lady?"

One of the boys gave it a quick glance.

"Nah, mate. I was in bed."

One of his friends giggled.

"Who with?"

"None of your fucking business."

Dan signalled to Jordan and they moved away.

"Let's ask the people in the swing park."

A harassed mother holding a whining toddler on her hip pushed an older child sitting on a swing.

"We're looking for this lady." Dan showed the photo to the woman. "Have you seen her?"

The toddler began to cry. The woman shrugged, pushed the child a little higher, whilst rocking the toddler back and forth.

"I might have done, I don't know. I was here on Sunday morning. There was a woman walking around the jogging track, but I'm not sure whether it was her or not."

"Thank you." Dan sighed. "Sorry to bother you."

He could tell Yvonne was in one of her moods as soon as he unlocked the front door.

"Somebody called Richard Jones rang just now. He was going to phone your mobile."

As he watched her stomp back into the living room his mobile phone buzzed.

"Mr Hayes?"

"Yes." Dan felt a frisson of anxiety run through him like a bolt of lightning.

"This is Richard Jones. Are you able to come down to the station as soon as possible please?

"Of course. Have you found Jill?"

"We might have some news, but you'll need to come to the station."

Dan felt uneasy.

"I'll come straight away."

He saw the change in his son's demeanour as soon as he ended the call.

"Where's Mum?" Jordan clamoured around him. "Have they found her?"

"I have to go to the station." Dan shook his head. "Just me. You stay here with Yvonne."

"No! I'm coming with you!"

"They only want *me*." Dan had a terrible foreboding. "You can't come."

"Well phone me then." Jordan sighed. "I'll be waiting."

Richard Jones hated to dash the hope in Dan Hayes' eyes, but it had to be done.

"I'm afraid there's no easy way to tell you this, but a man walking his dog in Daxton Woods found a body this afternoon which matches your ex-wife's description. We'd like you to come to the mortuary and identify whether or not it is Jill Hayes."

"Oh." Dan felt sick.

DI Jones scrambled for something to say.

"Would you like a tea or coffee?"

"No thanks, I just want to get on with it and get it over with."

With some trepidation Dan followed Richard Jones down a narrow corridor to the back of the building. The detective tapped in a code on the wide reinforced door and switched on a fluorescent light. Dan felt cold. He saw large grey metallic drawers with handles on one side, and a long metal table with side drainage areas on the other. His heart was pounding in his chest, and at that moment he wanted to be anywhere rather than in front of the drawer that was opening before his eyes.

"The chap found her propped up against a tree. She'd been strangled, but an autopsy needs to be done to confirm. I hope it's not your ex-wife, but we have to be sure."

Dan squeezed his eyes shut as the sheet was pulled back, exposing the body. He couldn't bear to look. Richard Jones' voice brought him out of denial.

"Mr Hayes?"

Reluctantly Dan came back to the present. Jill lay before him, an empty shell, soulless. He felt sick. He looked away from her face at her bare hands, usually festooned with rings.

"Yes, it's Jill." He swallowed hard. "Where are her effects?"

"There are some clothes, but nothing else."

"What about her rings?" Dan turned to DI Jones. "And she always wore the Rolex watch I gave her. Where is that?"

Richard Jones shook his head.

"There was nothing else on her body, no jewellery and no watch. I'm very sorry."

Chapter Twelve

He couldn't remember the last time he had cuddled his son.

Dan held Jordan tight and let his tears fall into the boy's auburn hair.

"I'm so sorry Jordie."

Jordan's voice shook with sobs.

"Are y-y-you sure it w-was her?"

"Positive." He whispered. "The police have now launched a murder inquiry. What Mum found out at the college cost her dearly."

Jordan broke into fresh sobs.

"What's going to happen to me?"

"I'll look after you like I've always done. You'll carry on at work, study at college, and live here with Yvonne and me."

"I-I don't want to go to that college!" Jordan's head shook from side to side.

"Then we can ask CoolingAid to send you to a different one. That's not a problem." Dan wiped his eyes with the back of his sleeve. "It'll all work out, don't worry."

"Yvonne doesn't want me here. I want to go home, Dad!"

His son was inconsolable. Dan held Jordan tight, aware that Yvonne was standing awkwardly in the bedroom doorway.

"You're only sixteen. You're not earning enough to run your own home yet. I'll rent out Mum's house for a couple of years while you do your apprenticeship, and then you can move back in when you're older. How does that sound?"

"O-okay." The voice was muffled against his shirt front.

Dan closed his eyes and sighed.

"How's Jordan? Is he okay?"

Dan looked at Yvonne and shrugged.

"He's asleep now. He's got to come to terms with it all in his own time."

"I don't think he likes me."

Dan hid a twinge of annoyance.

"Well, perhaps you'll have to work a bit more on *making* him like you."

"Wouldn't it be better if he lived with his grandparents?"

He wondered if he had heard her right. Dan sat up straighter in his armchair and stared at his wife.

"Tell me you're joking, right? My mum is too old, and Jill's parents live fifty miles away. He can't cycle to work from there! He's grieving for his mum for God's sake!"

He knew that once she had a bee in her bonnet about something, she would never let it rest.

"Sure he can stay a while, but I never wanted kids, Dan, especially somebody else's. You know that. We have to get this out in the open *now*."

"Jordan stays with me." Dan shook his head. "He's not going anywhere. He's sixteen and he needs his dad at the moment."

The silence was broken as Yvonne stood up.

"Well, excuse me for *living*!"

Dan flopped back in the chair and closed his eyes.

"Dad, you okay?"

Dan woke up with a start to find he was still in the armchair, with the front room in darkness. He turned his head to see Jordan framed in the doorway, the hall light illuminating his tousled hair.

"I fell asleep. What time is it?"

"Half past one. I came down to get a drink."

"I'll go up now. We'll bring the rest of your stuff over in the car when I get home from work later on."

"Okay."

He padded upstairs and quietly opened the bedroom door. Yvonne lay unmoving facing the wall. He quickly undressed and eased into bed beside her.

"You awake?"

There was no reply. Whether she was conscious or not he had no idea. He closed his eyes and waited for sleep to come. After a few moments he heard Jordan's footsteps on the stairs. It seemed strange having somebody else in the house apart from the two of them. He would have to get used to it.

After a week of it, the silent treatment was beginning to grate on his nerves. Dan had come to dread the evening mealtime when the three of them would sit around the table. He would attempt a conversation, but would end up just talking to Jordan instead about his day at work, and his irritation grew at his wife's obstinate refusal to welcome his son into the fold. When Jordan escaped upstairs as soon as he had eaten the last spoonful of pudding, Dan decided enough was enough. He helped himself to a yoghurt from the fridge and sat back down at the table.

"I have to say that you're being totally unreasonable about all this."

Yvonne shrugged.

"You *know* I never wanted kids of my own. It's an invasion of our privacy."

"His mother's been murdered!" Dan thumped the yoghurt pot on the table for extra effect. "Where the fuck else has he got to go?"

"Look, I'm sorry your ex-wife is dead, but you can't just foist a teenage boy on me and expect me to like it!" Yvonne stood up and began stacking plates in the dishwasher. "He hates the sight of me as well, which doesn't help."

Dan sighed.

"I don't blame him. All he's getting from you are negative vibes."

Yvonne slammed the dishwasher door closed.

"So you're on *his* side then?"

"Yeah." Dan nodded. "I am. The poor sod needs all the help he can get."

"Then what's the point of us going on? It's me or him Dan, make your choice."

"I'll move back in with Jordan for now." Dan stood up. "Then you'll be rid of both of us."

Chapter Thirteen

LINUS EWING

The formal flower beds were a treat for the eye. Linus inhaled the scent of roses as he entered Howard Davis Park and jogged towards George V's statue. His routine never wavered; six laps of the park, followed by a shower, and then breakfast with Helen and the children before overseeing the running of Accelerat from the comfort of his mahogany desk. Helen would drop the kids off at their private schools before returning home. Maybe they would swim in their pool or make love after lunch if he was lucky.

So when he pressed the code to open the security gates and saw an unknown car parked on the gravel, Linus's familiar routine suddenly took a nosedive. Curious, he jogged up the drive to the main door instead of walking and cooling off, eager to see the person whom his wife had allowed into their private enclave. He noticed Helen had already seen him coming, and had opened the front door. Behind her stood two well-built men in police uniform.

"Linus, these are Detective Inspector Richard Jones from the mainland, and Sergeant Tom Spicer from the Jersey Police Force."

Linus, hot and sweaty, shook the policemen's hands.

"Hi. What brings you both here today?"

Tom Spicer, the older of the two, spoke first.

"Just routine enquires."

Linus felt a twinge of unease.

"Come into my study."

He felt somehow at a disadvantage standing in front of Jones and Spicer in his running shorts and singlet, and wondered if this was the effect the policemen had intended to convey. However, he decided to bluster his way through whatever was going to be thrown at him.

"You're somewhat out of your jurisdiction aren't you Detective Inspector?"

Richard Jones kept eye contact.

"I'm investigating a murder, and I need your help with our inquiries."

"I'll do all I can, obviously." Linus hated the bastard on sight. "What would you like to know?"

"You're the Managing Director of Accelerat, the company that owns Starfaire and the Fideliter examinations board?"

"Yes, that's correct." Linus nodded.

"We're investigating the death of Mrs Jill Hayes, who worked at Daxton College in the Exams department."

Linus let a brief frisson of impatience cross his features.

"I'm sorry, I don't know this person. I've lived here in Jersey for fifteen years with my family. I very rarely visit the mainland."

"Shortly before she was murdered Mrs Hayes wrote letters to a local and national newspaper, and to the Starfaire exam regulatory board criticising some exam questions set by Fideliter."

"Desi Ingram at Starfaire has passed all Fideliter's exam questions as perfectly proper. Accelerat is a legally registered company, and I pay over a hundred thousand pounds in tax every year." Linus wanted the two detectives gone. "Now if you don't mind, I'm a busy man."

Tom Spicer wondered what kind of man would willingly undergo bleached blond highlights. He took a piece of paper out of his pocket.

"I have a search warrant here, Mr Ewing. Since you own both Accelerat, Starfaire and Fideliter, as part of our routine enquiries I need to take your computer away for investigation."

"This is an outrage!" Linus Ewing felt sweat dripping down his forehead into his eyes. "How dare you come into my home and accuse me of murder!"

"We're not accusing you of anything, Mr Ewing, but I will caution you not to leave Jersey while investigations are underway. Your computer will be returned to you as soon as it's possible to do so. We'll need your code to log in."

"And how will I work in the meantime?" Linus wanted to punch Tom Spicer into next week. "Any ideas?"

"You still have a telephone Mr Ewing."

Linus let out a snort as he scribbled down his password.

"You've probably already bugged it."

His knuckles made contact with the unforgiving tiles of the shower. Linus ignored rivulets of blood trickling down the wall and carried on punching until he could take no more pain. Then calmer, he towelled himself dry, donned his working garb of designer shirt and chinos, and went to his study to take a pre-paid mobile phone out from a hidden compartment in his desk.

"Des?"

"What?"

Her voice sounded drowsy. He imagined her naked and spread-eagled amongst the white satin sheets he knew so well.

"Can you meet me in the park by the coffee place in say, one hour?"

"Fuck off."

Despite his anger he let a brief smile play about his lips.

"Alright then, two hours."

He heard a yawn and a sigh.

"This had better be good."

"It is, believe me."

He ended the call on hearing his wife outside in the hallway. Linus hid the phone again, ran a comb through his hair, and opened the door. Helen looked past him into the study.

"I saw them carrying your computer out."

"Just routine they said." Linus shrugged. "It's a bloody inconvenience."

"What are they investigating?"

Linus hid his bloodied knuckles as best he could.

"Some woman's been murdered on the mainland. Why they think I've got anything to do with it I don't know! I haven't been off the Island for months!"

He saw her looking at him trying to gauge his overall mood. He slid his hands over his wife's shoulders and pulled her to him.

"Don't worry about it. I've got some business with Desi. I'll have to go out in a bit, but I'm sure the police will sort their problems out in a few days."

He hoped Helen couldn't feel how rapidly his heart was beating.

He grabbed a coffee from the kiosk and waited, his foot tapping impatiently against the table leg. He could not help but smile as, fashionably late, Desiree Ingram's size six figure came into view, causing heads to turn as she sashayed towards him as though strutting along an imaginary catwalk. She sat down carefully, after brushing a speck of dirt from her chair.

"What am I doing here? You know I never get up 'til two at weekends."

Linus drained his cup and stood up.

"Let's take a walk to somewhere a bit more private."

He touched her arm lightly and steered her in the direction of an empty chair by a brick wall festooned with colourful trailing plants in hanging baskets.

"Have you heard anything?"

Desiree let out a snort of laughter.

"Steven Finch is already in Brazil."

Linus let out a sigh of relief.

"He was paid in cash?"

Desiree nodded.

"Sure. I sorted it. I took the money out of the safety deposit box. It's not traceable. Don't get your knickers in a twist. He's happy – he thinks he's on a winner, and of course he *will* be until Carlos finds him. Trouble is, now I'm one man short."

"Advertise then." Linus let his fingers trail along Desiree's tanned arm. "Let's act normally. The police are sniffing round - we've got to be a bit more careful from now on. If you want to contact me, use the pre-paid phone I gave you. Don't send any emails."

"Too late, I already did." Desiree shrugged and a small smile played about her lips. "Just give us a kiss and shut up."

Chapter Fourteen

TOM SPICER

From his vantage point way across the other side of the park, Tom Spicer adjusted his zoom lens to obtain a clearer photo of the couple on the bench who were locked in a passionate embrace. The woman had her fingers entwined in Linus Ewing's bleached highlights, and Tom wondered who she was. When she broke away, Tom took another photo. Richard Jones tried to make out the woman's features.

"Do you recognise her?"

"No." Tom replied and clicked the camera again. "But I sure as hell am going to find out who Ewing's seeing on the side."

"Slimy bastard." Jones drew a breath. "He's probably in it up to his neck."

Tom stood up.

"Let's get back to base. I want to get these pictures developed and find out who she is."

Holding the still damp photos carefully, he peered over his assistant Ed Peters' shoulder.

"Found anything yet?"

"Not really." Ed sat back in his chair and yawned. "A pretty racy email came in for Ewing yesterday from somebody called Desi Ingram. Apart from that, nothing to report as yet."

"Desi Ingram?" Richard Jones took out his notebook and riffled through the first few pages. "Ewing mentioned a Desi Ingram as working for Starfaire, the exam regulatory board."

Tom nodded.

"Google *Desi Ingram* Ed, and see what comes up."

A fashionably thin and sartorially elegant carbon copy of the woman in the photo playing tonsil tennis with Linus Ewing popped up on the screen.

"Managing Director, eh?" Tom Spicer checked his photo once more to be sure. "Phone the number on the screen, Ed. I think we need to have a few words with Ms Ingram."

Tom spoke clearly into the security console.

"Tom Spicer and Richard Jones to see Desiree Ingram."

The gates rolled back and Tom drove slowly along a tree-lined drive towards a double fronted rectory-style Victorian manor house complete with double garage.

"Whatever she's doing, it's obviously paying quite well."

He could see her already waiting at the front porch for them, dressed in expensive looking designer clothes. Tom parked in front of the garages and kept eye contact as he and Jones walked towards her.

"Good afternoon Ms Ingram. I am Sergeant Tom Spicer from the Jersey Police, and this is Detective Inspector Richard Jones from Daxton."

"Daxton?" Desiree Ingram looked haughtily at Richard Jones. "Aren't you a bit out of your jurisdiction?"

"Apparently." Jones replied drily. "Can we come in?"

Desiree stood to one side and ushered them through unsmilingly.

"Be my guest."

Tom took in a substantial black and white tiled hallway with two squashy sofas, an antique coat stand, and a large open fireplace. Desiree remained standing.

"We might as well stay here, seeing as what I have to say probably won't take long."

Tom disliked the woman on sight.

"We're investigating the murder of Mrs Jill Hayes, which took place in Daxton recently."

He heard her sigh impatiently.

"And I'm supposed to know this lady?"

"That's what we've come here to ask you."

Desiree shrugged.

"I've never heard of her."

Tom decided to play his trump card.

"She wrote a couple of letters to the newspapers criticising some of Fideliter's exam questions. The questions wouldn't have bothered a five year old, let alone somebody aged sixteen. We're wondering why Starfaire would have approved them for general use."

He was pleased to see a momentary lapse of self-control on her features as she struggled for a reply.

"What kind of questions?"

Tom recognised that she was stalling for time. He produced a piece of paper from his pocket and held it out in front of her.

"Here's a copy of one of the exam papers. Students had to write down what they would keep in their kitchen cupboards. Another one asked what the capital of England is."

He watched the woman's face as she peered intently at it.

"I don't remember seeing anything like this. Are you sure it's an official exam paper?"

"Quite certain." Tom sighed with frustration. "After complaining about what she had seen to the newspapers, Mrs Hayes' son was then assaulted, and shortly after Mrs Hayes herself was murdered."

"Well, somebody from Starfaire must have passed it for use, but it wasn't me."

Tom put the paper back in his pocket.

"You're the MD. By the end of tomorrow I'll be expecting a phone call from you telling me who it was."

"Sure." Desiree shrugged. "I'll work on it."

Chapter Fifteen

HELEN EWING

Helen had noticed a sudden change in her husband. Linus was edgy, impatient with the children, and tended to shut himself away in the study for long periods of time. If she pressed her ear close to the door she could hear frustratingly muted one-sided phone conversations, but the tone of his voice had told her that he was speaking to a woman, as he had always sounded more strident if the caller was male. When she'd picked the right moment to mention his bloodied knuckles, he had told her to mind her own business.

She suspected her husband might be having an affair.

Beside herself with rage and grief that another woman could be trying to muscle in on her family and their comfortable lifestyle, she decided there was only one thing left to do; she must hire a private detective to find out exactly what her husband did when he left the house on his increasingly frequent errands.

There were pages of private detectives listed in the Yellowbook Directory. Helen decided to buy herself a pay-as-you-go mobile phone and do a little investigating herself.

The middle-aged man at her front door looked to be dressed too casually for a first time meeting with a new client, but Helen Ewing decided to give Eric Cubitt with his combat shorts and tee-shirt the benefit of the doubt.

"Mr Cubitt! Come in." Helen waved an arm in the direction of the hallway.

"Afternoon Ma'am." Eric Cubitt placed one designer trainer over the threshold. "Pleased to meet you."

"Don't call me Ma'am, *please*." Helen giggled whilst shaking her head. "You make me feel like the Queen."

Eric grinned and followed Helen into the house.

"All ladies are queens to me."

"I think we're going to get along splendidly." Helen entered the front room. "Do take a seat. We've got about an hour. My husband has taken the three younger children to their music lessons."

She watched Eric sitting down on the edge of the leather Chesterfield and taking a quick glance around the room before speaking.

"So… what can I do for you Mrs Ewing?"

Helen took a deep breath.

"The usual. I'd like to find out if my husband is having an affair."

"Ah…I see." Eric nodded. "Yes, I get a lot of those."

"I thought you might." Helen sighed. "I can give you a photo and a list of his usual haunts. You'll need to phone me on the number I called you on before."

"Sure. Here's my rates and terms and conditions." Eric peeled off a piece of paper from a booklet. "Have a read through and then if you're in agreement we can get to work."

From the window she watched the children rush straight out of the car and into the house, whilst Linus sat in the front seat talking on his phone. Helen went out into the hallway. Eleven year old Jack was the first to run past her on the way up to his room.

"Hi Mum!"

"How'd it go?" Helen called up the stairs to her son's retreating back.

"I can take grade one next month! Mrs Stephenson's put me in for it!"

"Great!"

Helen laughed and focused on Maria, five, and Callum, eight.

"Good lessons today, kiddies?"

"No." Callum threw his rucksack on the floor. "I don't want to play the stupid piano anymore. I want guitar lessons."

"I played *The Birthday Party*." Maria's high voice piped up. "Mrs Stephenson said I played it very well. I wanted Daddy to hear it, but he had to go out."

"It's *stupid*!" Callum gave Maria a kick. "*You're* stupid!"

"Mum, tell him!"

Helen felt Maria's little arms grab one of her legs, holding on for dear life.

"Callum, that's enough!" Helen's voice rose over her daughter's cries. "Maria, what do you mean, Daddy had to go out?"

She looked down at Maria, disentangled her arms, and picked her daughter up to sit squarely on her hip.

"Daddy got in the car and drove off while we were having our lessons. Mrs Stephenson was cross." Maria's eyes were still full of tears. "He came back when we were all finished. Mrs Stephenson told him she wasn't a babysitter."

Helen looked out onto the driveway to see Linus getting out of the car. She put Maria down onto the tiled floor.

"Emma's just come home from Keira's. Go up and see if she'll read you a story."

Hearing Maria's departing footsteps, Helen walked to the front door and pulled it to behind her just as Linus reached the porch.

"Where did you go when the kids were in their lessons? Maria said that Mrs Stephenson wasn't very pleased to be left alone with all of them."

She saw a brief flash of anger cross her husband's face as he pushed past her.

"I had business to see to! Why don't *you* take them if I'm such a shit father? You're only sitting here all day on your arse!"

"Because you said *you* wanted to!" Helen fought back the tears threatening to fill her eyes. "Linus, what *is* wrong with you?"

But he had already disappeared into his study, slamming the door in order to shut her out.

It was two weeks before she heard from Eric Cubitt again, but as usual he was on time. She glanced at his new pair of designer trainers, and felt sure her money must have paid for them. She noticed a thick folder under his arm, and wondered what he had found out.

"Mr Cubitt. Do come in."

"Cheers." Eric Cubitt wiped his feet. "Thanks to the long lens on my camera I now have the information you require."

She led him into the kitchen, her heart racing.

"Can I get you a drink?"

"No thanks, I won't stay long." He shook his head. "I'll get right to the point if I may.

"Please do." She sat down opposite him. "What have you got for me?"

"Well…" He opened the folder and pushed some photographs in her direction. "You're right in that your husband is having an affair if these are anything to go by."

She felt sick to her stomach as she forced herself to look at Linus and Desi Ingram. Her voice sounded feeble as she spoke.

"May I keep these?"

"Sure." He nodded. "I have copies."

Everything they had planned for and worked towards had now turned to dust, and she knew for certain that nothing could ever be the same between her and Linus again. Helen managed to wait until Cubitt was out of the door before letting bitter tears fall onto the photo of her husband and his mistress. Now she finally had proof of his infidelity, she would need to think very carefully about how she could use it to her advantage.

Chapter Sixteen

RICHARD JONES

Another cloudless day in paradise. Richard Jones finished shaving and looked at himself critically in the hotel's mirror, noticing a few more grey hairs and that his eyebrows had started to grow outwards. He sighed with the realisation of impending old age just as his mobile phone buzzed. He picked up the phone which he had placed on the cistern.

"Hello?"

"Richard, it's Sally. What's going on? Any leads yet?"

"Sal, you know I'm not really supposed to talk about it." Richard pulled out a stray eyebrow hair. "You're on sick leave."

"Bullshit!" Sally's voice came down the line clear and strong. "Jill was my friend. Stop pissing about and tell me what you know."

"Nothing really." Richard held the phone under his ear and pulled the plug out of the sink. "The MD and his mistress are slippery bastards. Apparently some guy who's conveniently left the company and the country authorised the examination questions while the two of them were at some kind of conference. It's all a load of bollocks if you ask me."

"This guy; are they going to advertise his job?"

"How do I know?" Richard yawned. "If there was a guy in the first place."

There followed a brief silence, before he heard her speak again

"There's only one thing for it, Rich."

His brain was on immediate alert.

"What?"

"I'll go undercover. If there's a vacancy at Starfaire I'll apply. Get your man over there to give me a new identity, a list of relevant qualifications, and a safe house. They won't know who I am. It'll be the desk job to end all desk jobs - I'm going loopy sitting here all day. I'll claim discrimination if they won't take on somebody disabled. They'll take me on to shut me up!"

"You're off sick!" Richard found he was shaking his head. "The chief will never approve."

"I'm not sick, and you know it." Sally's voice had risen a couple of semitones. "I'm just waiting for the right leg and the right desk job. Don't tell him and he'll never know. I'm still getting paid, so I want to work for my money. See what you can do."

"Bloody hell." Richard laughed. "You always did have guts, Sal."

"Shut up with the flattery, and get on with it. Work out which address I'll have to give though, and make it look good. Maybe I can give her yours, ha ha!"

Richard was still shaking his head as he ended the call.

He helped himself to a cup of coffee from the percolator.

"Morning!" Richard acknowledged Tom as he came in and stood behind him in the queue. "Can I run something by you?"

"Sure." Tom filled up his cup. "Come into my office and we can have a chat."

Richard waited until Tom had closed the door behind him.

"I've got a colleague – well, she's on sick leave at the moment. She's offering to go undercover at Starfaire and have a snoop around if you can give her a new identity, relevant exam passes, and a safe address."

He was aware Tom was looking at him with undisguised interest.

"Is she any good? What's the matter with her?"

"Yeah, she's good. She's waiting for a prosthetic leg and a desk job. Her right leg was amputated due to diabetes. Are Starfaire advertising any vacancies?"

Tom went over to his desk, picked up a newspaper, and sat down.

"Take a seat. Here's the local rag – I'll have a look."

He leafed through the back pages while Richard looked on impatiently.

"Yeah, here we are." Tom drew a black ring around the advert with a biro. "Administrator wanted at their St. Helier office, computer literacy essential. There's still another two weeks until the deadline, so I'll run it by my superiors. Perhaps it's the only real way to find out what's going on."

Richard peered over the desk at the advert.
"She'll have back up at all times?"
"Of course." Tom nodded. "I'll guarantee that."
Richard sat back in his chair and took a sip of coffee.
"Let's get the ball rolling then."

Chapter Seventeen

SALLY DAVIDGE

Sally took an instant dislike to Desi Ingram as she sat peering at her with undisguised interest from the other side of a well-polished mahogany desk.

"So…Ms Trent… Liz. Can I call you Liz?"

"Sure." Sally nodded. "Everybody does."

"Tell me a bit about yourself. Why have you applied for this post?"

"I may be in a wheelchair, but I can still work." Sally shrugged her shoulders. "And I can drive, as long as someone can get my wheelchair in and out of the car. The car is specially adapted. I've recently re-located back to Jersey to be near my parents, and have always done office work. As you can tell from my CV, I'm well qualified for the job."

"So I see." Desi flipped idly through the carefully prepared pages. "Liz…what do you consider are your strengths and weaknesses?"

Sally hated the same old question that popped up at every bloody job interview.

"I'm organised and reliable, and was office manager at my last job. My weakness is that I've only got one leg, but I don't let that stop me."

Desi's shrill laugh grated on Sally's ears.

"Good for you! I can tell you're a fighter! There's security guy at the front desk who can help with your wheelchair. When can you start?"

Sally managed to hide her surprise.

"Straight away. How about Monday?"

"Done." Desi leaned over the desk and held out her right hand. "Look forward to having you on board."

As Sally shook the small, manicured hand, she smiled sweetly and notched up a point on her virtual scoreboard; Liz Trent 1, Desi Ingram 0.

Sally adjusted the computer monitor and wondered if the previous user had been at least seven feet tall. Beside her Desi Ingram shifted impatiently.

"To start with I'm going to put you in charge of organising inspections and typing up inspectors' reports."

"Fine." Sally nodded. "I assume on the mainland as well as in Jersey?"

"That's right. You'll need to get familiar with our in-house system though. Your predecessor would have saved a list of our inspectors, and you'll be able to see which institution they last went to and when. It's our policy to only give a couple of days' notice of when an exams inspection is going to take place."

"Who was my predecessor by the way?" Sally hoped she looked sufficiently dumb.

"Oh, Steven Finch." Desi shrugged. "He moved abroad. Now I've got into the system, you'll have to put your own password in. Take some time sifting through the computer and getting familiar with the files. Choose schools where there hasn't been an inspection for at least two years."

"Okay."

Desi stood up.

"But first I think you'd better introduce yourself to our inspectors. Find out where they live, and then you'll know which areas they prefer and which schools to send them to. All their details have been inputted by Finch."

Sally looked at Desi's tiny retreating back, and felt huge and lumbering in comparison. Something about the woman rubbed her up the wrong way, and she was determined to find out what it was.

Sally lifted the teapot in Richard's direction.

"Another cup of tea, Rich?"

"Not for me thanks." Richard raised one hand. "How's the new job going?"

"I've found out that Starfaire have ten inspectors for the Fideliter board. All their previous reports are glowing regarding whichever schools they've visited, but Daxton College hasn't had an inspection for about three years as far as I can tell."

"So you're going to send someone out there?" Richard looked at her with interest.

"I think I might just do that." Sally grinned. "Time to give Nicola Scott a ring."

Richard helped himself to a biscuit.

"Who's she?"

"Apparently the inspector for that area." Sally poured herself a second cup. "According to the computer anyway. It'll be interesting to see what she thinks of the exam questions."

Richard nodded.

"What about Desi Ingram?"

"I haven't made my mind up about her yet." Sally took a sip of tea. "There's something about her that doesn't sit right with me."

"You and me both." Richard shot Sally a conspiratorial wink. "Keep on digging, Sal. You're doing a grand job."

"Nicola Scott?

Sally could hear a radio playing loudly in the background. A young female voice replied with a strong South London accent.

"My mum's out at the moment, but her surname's not Scott anymore."

Sally strained to hear the girl's reply over the sound of an electric guitar.

"What is it then?"

"Bream – it's her maiden name. She's just got divorced."

"I'll call back." Sally tried to reach her notebook with one hand but gave up. "Thanks."

She ended the call and reached down into her handbag, impatiently riffling through the notebook until she found the name she was looking for…

John Bream – Principal of Daxton College.

Sally raised an arm as Desi strolled nonchalantly by.

"You have a question, Liz?" Desi looked enquiringly at Sally.

"Yeah." Sally nodded. "Do you know Nicola Scott?"

"We speak sometimes. I interviewed her years ago when she applied to work for Starfaire. She lives over on the mainland."

"Is she related to the principal of Daxton College by any chance?"

There was the briefest of pauses that did not go unnoticed by Sally, before Desi shrugged her shoulders.

"Not that I know of. Why?"

Sally opened her notebook again.

"Just wondered. Apparently she's divorced and has reverted back to her maiden name, which is the same as the principal's."

Desi's smile did not quite reach her eyes.

"Coincidence probably."

"Sure." Sally replied.

She saw the first handwritten report for typing up in her in-tray early on a Monday morning about a month later. Sally noticed the envelope had already been opened, although it had been addressed to her. As she booted up the computer, she had a quick glance through the glowing report of Daxton College's exams system. Sally hooted out a wry laugh.

Nicola Bream had excelled herself.

Chapter Eighteen

DESI INGRAM

The woman, carrying a little girl on her hip, was dressed a low cut top and tight fitting leggings, accentuating her undulating flesh in a most unattractive way. Desi made a herculean effort not to wrinkle her nose, and curbed her urge to slam the office door in the woman's face.

"What can I do for you?"

The toddler began to whine. The woman put the girl down, then took a biscuit from her bag and put it in the child's pudgy hand.

"I'm Maddy Kirk, Steven's partner. I want to know where he is. He's been gone for days, and I can't get him on his mobile."

Desi smiled through a sudden heartsink moment.

"He's in Brazil on business. Didn't he tell you?"

"He didn't tell me anything." Maddy Kirk shook her head. "All he said was that he had to go abroad for a couple of days. It's been more than that. What's he doing out there?"

A mental image of Steven washed up face down on Ipanema Beach's incoming tide surrounded by screaming thong-clad beauties came to mind. Desi sighed with a marked impatience to rid herself of two inconveniences to Steven's past life that now stood before her.

"He's probably just out of range or something."

Maddy fixed an unswerving gaze on Desi.

"No, something isn't right. I've always been able to get him on the phone or by email before, or he's usually called me."

Desi shrugged.

"Sorry. He'll be home when he's finished his assignment."

"He'd better be." Maddy replied with a touch of venom. "Or I'm going to the police to report him missing."

Desi, somewhat worried, watched Madeline Kirk turn on her worn-down heel and walk away.

She could never resist him. Desi, sated and slightly out of breath, rolled off Linus and curled up by his side.

"You know you're a bastard, don't you?"

Linus chuckled and kissed the top of her head.

"Of course. I'm going to hell in a handcart."

She ran her fingers through the thick matting of hair on his chest.

"Finch's wife, girlfriend or whatever, came to the office the other day."

Linus propped himself up on one elbow, raised an eyebrow, and looked at her.

"Have you shagged me so I'm in a good mood when you break bad news?"

"Absolutely." She laughed. "If she doesn't hear from him, then I think she'll go to the police."

She put her face into his chest, smelt the maleness of him, and wished the world would go away. His deep voice vibrated through her closed eyelids.

"Let her go. As you probably know, they'll never get a word out of him. Look, I've got to go." He ruffled the top of her head, pushed her away and swung his legs over the side of the bed. "You can't keep me here any longer, you little temptress, you…"

Naked, she lay back against the pillows, then flashed him a smile and opened her heart.

"I love you, Linus. You know that, don't you?"

"Sure." He nodded. "When the kids are older, then we'll be together."

She knew with some certainty never to believe a single word that came out of his mouth. She sighed; she was sick of his platitudes and being strung along like a lovesick teenager. She needed to up the game a little bit to see where she really stood in his affections, and an old boyfriend from her teenage years, Dave Yuill, still kept in touch and thought the sun shone out of her porthole.

After she heard his engine roar along the drive and out the gates she threw on a dressing gown and picked up her pay-as-you-go mobile. She knew the number by heart.

"Ola!"

Raul Martinez sounded happy. She breathed a sigh of relief.

"You got the money then?"

"Si. I thank you from the bottom of my 'art."

Desi chuckled.

"Where is our friend?"

"He sleeps with the fishes."

"Have you been watching *The Godfather*?" Desi roared. "I trust the Atlantic is not too cold for our friend."

"He's enjoying the swim."

The line went dead. Desi flopped back down onto the bed, sated, but aware that Linus had caused a deep ache in her heart which would not go away. She turned over on her front and buried her face in the pillow that still smelt of him, and came to the conclusion that something needed to be done, and quickly, regarding Mr Linus Eden Ewing.

Chapter Nineteen

HELEN EWING

It was time to confront him. Helen shook with nerves and suppressed anger as she reached into the back of her wardrobe and took out copies of two photos that she knew Linus would not be happy to see. After checking all four children were sound asleep, she strode purposefully downstairs to the front room where her husband lay sprawled in front of the TV.

"Can we talk please, Linus?" She stood in front of him and tried not to make her voice wobble. "I need to speak to you about something."

Guarded and instantly suspicious, Linus sat up slowly and stared at the paperwork in her hand as he pressed the mute button on the TV's remote control. The Grandfather clock boomed out nine sonorous chimes, which to Helen sounded like a death knell.

"What's up?"

“These” She waved the photos in front of his face. “Obviously you and Desi are more than just good friends.”

Her Pyrrhic victory was short and unsatisfying as she watched the colour drain from his face. He shrugged.

“It was just a one night stand. It doesn’t mean anything.”

“Well, it means a lot to me!” Helen sat down quickly before her legs gave way. “I’ve been a loyal wife to you. I gave up my career to bring up your children, and this is how you repay me?”

Rattled and irritated, Linus stood up and towered over her.

“So you’ve had a private dick watching me then?”

“Too bloody right!” She nodded. “And I’m not as stupid as I look! The affair’s been going on for a lot longer than one night.”

Her heart felt as though it might pound out of her chest. Helen steadied her breath and inched along the settee away from him.

“It’s over now.” More in control, he sat down beside her. “It really was just a fleeting thing.”

Helen shook her head.

“I want *out*. You’ve ruined it for us! I never want sex with you again, or to sleep in a bed next to you. I can’t compete with *her*, nor would I want to.”

She got to her feet and walked towards the door, then turned around to face him.

“You’re going to have to provide for me and the children. I want a divorce. I’ll find a solicitor first thing in the morning, but for now I’ll move into one of the other bedrooms.”

There was no reply. Relieved and trembling, Helen hoped her shaky legs would carry her up the stairs to the top floor.

She was wide awake, with thoughts that raced around her head. Around midnight she crept down to the first floor and padded along the galleried landing past the closed door of their old bedroom, and then on down the back stairs to the kitchen. She blinked as the spotlights picked out Linus's shape stooped over a steaming cup at the breakfast bar. He looked up at her and gave a wry smile.

"I couldn't sleep either."

The kettle was still hot. Helen made herself a cup of tea and yawned.

"Perhaps it's your guilty conscience keeping you awake."

"Yeah, perhaps it is." Linus replied. "I'm sorry. I'm just an arsehole of the highest order."

She took a sip of tea.

"I can only agree. Well, you and Desi won't have to sneak around anymore. With a bit of luck she'll let you move in with her."

Tears welled up in the back of her eyes, but she refused to let them fall.

"You and the kids can have the house." Linus replied with a heavy sigh. "It's the least I can do. I'll see you're all well looked after."

He also looked near to tears. She hated the sight of him.

"Thank you. I'll take my tea back to bed."

It was only when she reached the safety of the spare room and locked the door did she let hot tears fall. A rush of emotions; anger, sadness, and a numb certainty that she was just not good enough made her wonder through her tears how long he had been cheating. Helen closed her eyes and thought about how she might break the news to the children. She dozed fitfully, and at some point during the night thought she heard Linus outside on the landing.

Chapter Twenty

SALLY DAVIDGE

"How are you settling in, Liz?"

With some relief Sally noticed the thin one dressed for outdoors.

"Fine thanks, Desi." She smiled through gritted teeth. "I'm really enjoying the job."

Desi had been bugging her for days; looking over her shoulder and generally overseeing every single thing she did. However, Sally could see that at last her employer might finally be letting the leash out a bit. Desi gave a thumbs up sign.

"I'm off out for a while. Can you take any messages for me please? Also Tattingwell College needs to be inspected."

"I'm already on the case." Sally nodded. "I'll sort it out this afternoon."

Desi walked towards the door.

"Thanks. I'll see you tomorrow."

She watched out of the window until Desi's car had disappeared off the forecourt and then wheeled herself back to the computer, eager to check her Hotmail account for any updates from Tom Spicer or Richard. She typed 'Hotmail' into the Google search engine, and was surprised to see Steven Finch's email address and password in dot form come up as soon as she had mistakenly typed the first letter of her name into the signing in box.

"What?"

Excited at this new discovery, Sally clicked on 'sign in', and quite to her surprise found herself looking at Steven's 54 new inbox messages, most of them she could see had been sent by a Madeline Kirk and had '*Where are you?*' or '*Why haven't you answered my email*?' in the subject boxes. She scrolled down the page and read a message from a Raul Martinez that had already been opened:

'I await the goods. Bring it tomorrow to 528 Rua San Luca, Ipanema.'

The email was dated a week before. Sally made a note of the man's name and address and had a quick check through a few other emails but could find nothing of note. She logged out, and then set up a new account and typed *LizTrentt01@hotmail.co.uk* and a new password into the Hotmail signing in box, before rattling off messages to Tom Spicer and Richard Jones.

At last a computer had been delivered to her safe house. Sally, impatient to get online, watched Bill Crathie set up her link to the outside world.

"Sorry Sally, there was a problem with it and we had to wait for a part." Bill switched on the computer, which roared into life. "You're all set to go now."

Sally nodded.

"Cheers Bill, I didn't want to use the work computer anymore … too risky. Do you want a cup of tea or coffee before you go?"

"No, it's okay. I'll see myself out." Bill gave her a wave with one hand. "Got to get back to the grindstone."

Sally wheeled herself over to the computer desk as she heard the front door close, pleased to discover that logging on to Hotmail was now somewhat quicker than at Starfaire. Her message to Tom Spicer had been read almost immediately, and he had sent a reply only one day ago.

'*Hi, will check out the address you gave me. I'll come and see you after work tomorrow, and we can have a chat.*'

Tomorrow was today, and she had finished work. Sally wheeled herself back to the window, surprised to see Tom chatting to Bill Crathie on her driveway. She rolled her wheelchair along the hallway and opened the door.

"Hi Tom!" Sally waved at the two men. "Come in when you're ready. I'll put the kettle on."

Two cups of steaming tea were on the kitchen table by the time Tom's large frame filled the kitchen doorway.

"What can you tell me?" Sally looked up at Tom. "Where's Richard?"

"Winging his way to Ipanema to check out that name and address you gave us with the help of Luiz Mendoza and his team from the Brazilian police. Probably a false name of course, but let's see what transpires."

"Sure." Sally chuckled. "Whoever gives their real name to a Hotmail account?"

"Of course." Tom nodded. "Ms Ingram's none the wiser, I take it?"

Sally shrugged.

"She's still calling me *Liz* if that's any comfort."

Tom sat down and took a noisy gulp of tea.

"You're doing well but don't worry, we'll get you out quickly if it looks as though things are going down the toilet."

"This whole exam business stinks." Sally sighed. "It's the kids I feel sorry for, and people like Jill. They're just pawns in the game of money and power. If it wasn't for Jill we'd never have found out about all this."

Tom slapped the palm of his hand on the table and leaned forward, looking intently at Sally.

"We'll get the bastards. Mark my words – we'll get them."

Sally nodded.

"On another tack, what about a cleaner for this place? As you can see, it's a bit difficult for me to run around with a hoover."

"I'll ask Fiona to come and see you. She's our lady who cleans the offices." Tom replied. "She might like a bit of extra money. I'll also instruct one of our men to keep a watchful eye on this place. Don't worry, you won't know he's about."

"Cheers." Sally smiled. "I feel better already."

Chapter Twenty-One

LINUS EWING

Her perplexed expression irritated him. He swung the heavy rucksack off his back and stepped into the hallway.

"Linus … what are you doing here?"

"Helen had me followed. She found out about us." Linus pushed past Desi. "Can I stay here with you for a bit?"

"No, actually." Desi, still in her bathrobe, placed herself in front of him. "It's not convenient at the moment."

He frowned.

"What the hell do you mean, it's not convenient? Who the fuck set you up in this house in the first place?"

He side-stepped her, kicked the rucksack further into the hallway and marched towards the front room, stopping in surprise at the sight of a good-looking young blond-haired man clad in the bathrobe that *he*, Linus, usually wore, and who lay slouched in an armchair with both bare feet up on a coffee table.

"Who the hell are *you*?" Linus looked at the man and then back to Desi. "Who's he?"

Desi wrapped the robe more tightly around her body.

"Oh, this is Dave, a friend. Dave, meet Linus."

"Charmed I'm sure." Dave gave Linus a languorous wave. "But as you can see, we're not really ready for company this afternoon."

Linus regarded Desi with undisguised venom.

"You'll have plenty of time to get to know Dave even better than you do now. I'm giving you a week's notice to pack your stuff, get out of here, and hand everything at Starfaire over to Liz. You're *out*."

He saw with some satisfaction a momentary frisson of panic wash over her features, before the usual mask of aloofness clamped down.

"Well, I've got a week then … so get out of my house!"

"Pleasure." Linus turned on his heel. "Some friends of mine will check that this house is empty next Sunday evening."

Desi walked up to him and looked him square in the eyes.

"And they'd better be friendly too, if I'm still packing. Don't forget I know all about your *business*, and if they're not… who knows what I might let slip to Dave in the heat of the moment?"

His hands balled into fists. Linus took a deep breath.

"I'll see myself out."

He picked up his discarded rucksack in the hallway and let the front door slam as hard as he could.

"Daddy!" Maria ran up to him and threw her arms around him. "Mummy said you'd gone away!"

"No darling." Linus hugged her. "I'm just here for a few more days, but we'll still see each other, don't worry."

He wanted to cry as he held the small form of his daughter. He gave a thin smile to Helen over the top of Maria's head, who had come out into the hallway.

"Linus, what are you doing here?"

"The place I was moving into fell through." He kissed the top of Maria's head. "I'll sort something out tomorrow."

"So ...*she* didn't want you either then?" Helen shot him a look of utter contempt. "Come to think of it... I don't blame her. And don't think you're sleeping in with me tonight!"

"Of course not." Linus replied gently. "I'll take one of the spare rooms."

He hadn't felt the need to smoke for a long time. Linus, clad only in pyjama bottoms, leaned out of the spare room window and struck a match to light his fourth cigarette in the space of an hour. The room smelt like Smoky Joe's and he knew Helen would give him a bollocking the next morning, but Linus at that particular moment did not care. Three of his children now did not speak to him, his wife wanted a divorce, and his lover preferred Dave without *his* bathrobe. Linus took a long drag on his cigarette and was too deep in gloom to hear the bedroom door creak open.

"The whole landing stinks of smoke."

With the cigarette still between his lips he turned around to face her, standing wraith-like in a white nightdress.

"Life's gone a bit pear shaped recently."

He swung back to the window and exhaled.

"And whose fault is that?" Helen replied with some force.

"Spare me the lecture." Linus rested his elbows on the window sill and watched the glow of his cigarette in the darkness. "Don't worry, as soon as I've sorted a place out I'll go."

"Maria still wants to see you."

Linus felt a small stab of pleasure suffuse his body.

"At least somebody does." He replied drily. "Of course I'll keep in touch with her, and any of the others too if they change their minds."

Helen nodded.

"What's happening with you and Desi?"

He took another drag of his cigarette.

"Not a lot. She's got somebody else now."

"I'm sure there'll soon be a whole queue of women ready to throw their knickers at you." Helen stated abruptly. "You won't have long to wait."

The bedroom door closed with a click. Linus sighed and exhaled smoke into the night.

Chapter Twenty-Two

SALLY DAVIDGE

She could tell straight away that all was not right in Desi's world. Nonetheless, she decided to begin the week on a happy note.

"Happy Monday, Desi." Sally wheeled herself to her desk. "Did you have a nice weekend?"

"Not particularly."

The curt reply cut off further avenues of conversation. Sally gave Desi a thin smile, switched on her computer, and wracked her brain to think of something else to say.

"I'll concentrate on sorting out a visit to Trimmingham College this morning, shall I?"

"Er… you'll be doing a bit more than that."

"Oh?" Sally looked up at Desi with interest.

"Like…learning how to take over my job for starters."

Sally realised just in time that her mouth was hanging open. She quickly regained her equilibrium and gave a nonchalant shrug.

"Whatever you like. Any particular reason why?"

"Yeah." Desi momentarily pursed her lips. "That bastard Linus Ewing has decided I'm no longer required. How are you with sending invoices and doing accounts?"

"I can learn." Sally replied with what passed for eagerness. "Will there be somebody to take over my job?"

Desi shook her head.

"Not unless Linus employs someone. He'll do all the hiring and firing now for Fideliter and Starfaire, as well as for Accelerat."

"Busy boy." Sally mused. "Well, what can I say? Sorry you're leaving."

Desi shrugged.

"There'll be a lot to learn this week. Hope you're up to it."

"Of course." Sally replied with a confidence she did not feel. "You can count on me."

She could hardly wait to get home. Sally opened her front door and wheeled herself along the small hallway and entered her front room. She reached round to the wheelchair's handle and unhooked her handbag, taking out a key from a small zipped pocket which fitted exactly into the lock on her desk's top drawer. She picked up a pay-as-you-go mobile phone from the drawer, and tapped in a number she now knew by heart.

"Hello."

"Hello yourself." Sally smiled. "How's it going, Richard?"

"I'm surrounded by bronzed beauties in thongs wherever I look."

Sally roared.

"What a nightmare! Any luck with Raul?"

She heard car horns in the background and a babble of voices before she heard Richard's voice again.

"We're staking out the place with a few of the Brazilian police for company. Nobody there at the moment."

"Keep me informed." Sally replied. "Meanwhile, all is not hunky-dory in the land of Starfaire."

"Oh? Tell me more!"

She imagined Richard hanging onto her every word at the other end.

"Desi's got the sack. I'm taking over her job starting next week. I'm going to try and stick my nose in Fideliter's business and take a look at the exam questions if I can."

"Bloody hell!" Richard's throaty laugh filtered down the phone line. "You don't waste much time, do you?"

Sally grinned.

"Nothing to do with me. She's obviously done something to piss the head honcho off."

"Keep your eyes and ears open, Sal."

"Will do. Let me know when Raul turns up."

She ended the call just as the doorbell rang. Sally wheeled herself back along the hallway, into the front room, and peeped through the curtain to see a middle aged lady standing patiently on the porch. When she opened the door she was greeted with a beaming smile.

"Hello, I'm Fiona Cook. Tom Spicer told me you're looking for a cleaner? I've just finished my housekeeping duties at the police station."

"Oh! Nice to meet you – I'm Sally!" Sally reversed the chair and ushered the woman in. "Come through, and we can have a chat."

It was a Deja-vu moment, although Fiona, with her matronly figure and close-cropped mousy-coloured hair hardly resembled Jill Hayes at all. Sally peeped outside briefly before closing the front door, but if there was an officer on guard she rapidly came to the conclusion that he was excellent at camouflage.

Chapter Twenty-Three

RICHARD JONES

Richard yawned and rubbed his eyes; *stakeouts seemed harder as age crept in and sleep became more desirable.* Even at 2am the Rua San Luca bustled with tourists and young bronzed people out for a good time. He rapidly came to the conclusion that with all the noise, sleep might have been impossible anyway.

From his vantage point behind a large truck Richard could keep number 528 in view, but the door had remained firmly closed for five days. Luiz Mendoza and his team hadn't had much luck either. Richard settled down in the seat of his car ready for another fruitless night.

However, around the time that tired partygoers began to drift homewards, Richard became aware that a large 4x4 silver Mercedes had slid into a parking space a little further along the opposite side of the road. Instantly alert, he followed the driver and a female companion with his eyes as they crossed over and hurried along the pavement towards number 528. The man, bearded and wearing an obvious designer suit, held the door open for his companion, whose long dark hair fell forward to hide her face as she tottered up the steps wearing dangerously high heels.

Richard picked up his mobile phone and searched for Luiz Mendoza's contact details. A sleepy voice answered almost immediately.

"Alô."

"Luiz, it's Richard Jones. We've got some activity at Rua San Luca. Looks like our Raul might have finally arrived. I'll make a note of the car's registration number."

"I'm on my way. I'll let the team know. Keep watching. We'll be there in about thirty minutes."

Lights blazed from the front of the house. Richard, now more wide awake than he had felt for days, checked the Mercedes' registration number with a pair of binoculars. When a dark van pulled up behind him, he stepped out of his car and walked up to where Luiz and five other police officers in riot gear, all armed and two carrying a battering ram, were in the process of quietly emerging from the van onto the street. After a whispered word from Luiz, three officers disappeared down a side alley next to the house. Luiz indicated with a thumb in the direction of the alley.

"They'll block the back door."

Richard nodded.

"What's the plan?"

"We'll use the *aríete* to announce our presence." Luiz whispered. "The search warrant's still valid. With a bit of luck we'll have a result tonight."

Sweating with anticipation, Richard moved in behind Luiz and the two officers carrying the battering ram. His heart thudded in disjointed rhythm to the sound of the battering ram against the door of 528 Rua San Luca.

"Polícia! fique onde você está!"

Upstairs, a woman screamed. Luiz and his team took the stairs two at a time, with Richard in close pursuit. A male, half naked and holding a pistol, ran out onto the landing and took in the unwelcome sight of three machine guns trained at his head. Luiz shouted.

"Largue a arma!"

The pistol fell to the floor with a thud, and the man held up his hands. Luiz, after handcuffing the man, spoke on the radio to his team members at the back door who entered the house and began to search the downstairs rooms. Richard walked into the main bedroom, where a woman sat fully clothed and ashen faced on the bed.

"I'm a police officer. Do you understand English?"

"Yes."

The woman's voice was sulky. Richard's eyes took in the expensively furnished room, the water bed, satin sheets, and walk-in wardrobes stuffed with designer gear.

"Mind if I have a look around?"

She looked at him with hate in her eyes.

"Yes, but hey, you're going to do it anyway, aren't you?"

Richard shrugged and began a search of the closets containing rack after rack of chic attire. Cupboards and drawers yielded nothing, and he felt uncomfortable riffling through the woman's underwear with its owner's eyes burning into his back.

"Getting your rocks off?"

Richard bit his tongue.

"Stand up, please. I want to look under the mattress."

As the woman got to her feet, a ray of illumination from an overhead spotlight bounced from her bracelet into Richard's line of vision. A recent conversation with Dan Hayes came to the forefront of his mind, and he glanced more closely at her wrist.

"Let me have a look at that, please."

Within the gold and stainless steel bracelet lay the face of a Rolex watch. With reluctance the woman handed it to him and he turned it over, ignoring shouts from officers on the floor below. On the back of the watch he read the inscription:

'To Jill on your 30th birthday. All my love, Dan.'

He stared at the woman.

"Where did you get this?"

The woman shrugged.

"I don't know."

Richard shook his head.

"Not good enough. What's your name?"

"Elaina Silva."

"Well, Elaina, Officer Mendoza will need to have a chat with you at the station about this."

"Raul gave it to me." Elaina volunteered, somewhat more agreeable. "I don't know where he got it from."

Richard beckoned Luiz Mendoza into the room, who was speaking in rapid Portuguese on his radio. "Luiz, this lady was wearing Jill Hayes' watch."

"They've found several kilos of cocaine in the basement." Luiz took the watch and inspected it. "My guys have arrested Raul. We'll grab his computer. Looks like this little lady will be accompanying him."

"I don't know anything else!" Elaina's voice held a note of panic. "You must believe me!"

"Elaina." Richard's tone was gentle. "Did Raul recently pay a visit to the U.K? Tell me what you know and you won't need to go to the station."

"He's been here with me."

"He hasn't been to the U.K?"

"No." Elaina replied, more forcefully. "I already said."

Richard looked intently at Elaina.

"We can check flight lists to make sure you're telling the truth."

Elaina shrugged.

Luiz took a set of handcuffs from his belt and fastened them around Elaina's wrists, who struggled in protest.

"Go to hell!" Elaina spat. "I don't know anything else!"

"Yeah, I probably will." Luiz pulled her towards him. "You're coming with us for now, little lady. It's going to be a long night."

Chapter Twenty-Four

RICHARD JONES

The man had a belligerent look about him. Richard, in his unhurried way, sat down opposite Raul Martinez, who tapped his fingers impatiently on the table.

"So … I've had my fingerprints taken. What else? When can I go home?"

Luiz Mendoza laughed from his vantage point by the door.

"Detective Jones is investigating a murder. Your girlfriend was wearing the murdered woman's watch. When you tell us how she came to be wearing it, then we can move on from there."

"I found it on Ipanema Beach."

"Somebody just casually drops a four thousand pound watch on the beach and walks away?"

Raul shrugged.

"Maybe they took it off to go swimming, and it got covered in sand …then they couldn't find it."

"Very convenient." Richard leaned back in his chair. "Officer Mendoza will be speaking to you about the cocaine, but I'm trying to get to the bottom of who murdered Jill Hayes."

Raul shook his head.

"I am not a murderer, Detective."

The door to the interview room opened, and Luiz Mendoza listened intently to a whispered message from a team member before striding across towards Richard.

"Raul, or should I say Carlos Iglesias?"

Raul jumped slightly at the name before resuming his usual impassive expression. Luiz Mendoza carried on.

"Your fingerprints match one hundred percent to Carlos Iglesias' prints. I must say, the beard and longer hair are a good disguise. I pulled you in a couple of years' ago."

"I want to phone my lawyer. NOW." Carlos folded his arms. "No comment."

Elaina Silva leaped up from her chair as soon as he walked through the door.

"I've told you all I know!"

"Yes." Richard nodded. "I'm sure you have. However, there's a few other questions I want to ask you."

He sat down opposite her.

"Please Ms Silva… do take a seat."

She slumped back into her chair and sighed. Richard switched on a voice recorder and announced the time, date, his own name and that of the interviewee.

"Did you know Raul is really Carlos Iglesias, who has previously been arrested on drugs' charges and also armed robbery?"

"No." Elaina looked up at him with interest. "I haven't known him very long."

Richard pulled a trump card.

"If you help us with our enquiries, then I am more likely to stop this interview so that you can go back home to bed."

Elaina twisted the watch around and around on her wrist.

"He … he has a bad temper. He gave me the watch to tell me he was sorry."

Richard leaned forward in his seat.

"Sorry for what?"

Elaina lifted up swathes of hair from both sides of her face to expose fading bruises on her neck.

"For these."

Richard looked with distaste at the yellowing marks.

"Ms Silva, did Raul, or Carlos to use his real name, take a recent flight to the UK?"

"No." Elaina shook her head again. "But he met with somebody here who *is* English. He called him Steve. I heard them talking in the house one night when I got up to use the bathroom. I think Raul may have bought the watch from Steve, because he gave it to me when he came upstairs. We'd had an argument."

"Where is Steve now?" Richard looked earnestly at Elaina. "Have you seen him? His partner has not heard from him, which is unusual as far as she is concerned."

"I don't know where he is. I only saw him briefly from the upstairs landing, he was sitting on a sofa in the front room." Elaina shrugged. "Can I go now?"

"Yes, really soon." Richard picked up the voice recorder. "You've been most helpful. I'll get a photo of Steven Finch faxed over to see if you can identify him before you go home."

"Sally?"

He could hear a yawn at the other end.

"Is that you, Richard? It's five o'clock in the bloody morning!"

Richard could have kicked himself.

"Shit! Sorry Sal, there's been a bit of a development I think."

"That's strange."

"What do you mean?" Richard asked impatiently.

"I've just got out of bed, and my cleaner's sitting on a bench in the front garden."

"Perhaps she wants to start the hoovering early."

"What's been going on, Rich?"

Richard smiled to himself whilst wondering whether Fiona Cook might be the only cleaner who had ever carried a gun.

"Looks like Steven Finch might have had dealings with a Carlos Iglesias, who's got previous here for armed robbery and drugs. Carlos gave Jill Hayes' watch to his girlfriend as a present, and the girlfriend thinks he might have bought it from an Englishman called Steve."

"So if it *is* Steven Finch who had the watch, then that could possibly track it back to Starfaire, Accelerat, and the Linus and Desi duo?"

"Exactly." Richard replied. "You should have been a detective."

A throaty laugh could be heard at the other end of the line.

"I am, you bugger! Can the girlfriend identify him?"

"She just has. She's certain it's the guy who was in her front room. We're going to keep our friend Carlos a while longer. The guys are checking his computer as we speak."

"Great. I'm going outside to ask my cleaner why she's sitting in the garden."

Chapter Twenty-Five

The constant smell of cigarettes on the upstairs landing was grating on her nerves. Helen tapped on the door to the room where Linus had seemingly ensconced himself. Smoke wafted into her nostrils when he opened the door.

"This can't go on, Linus. You're supposed to be moving out. The children are confused when they still see you at the dinner table."

She noticed the lack of personal hygiene. He hadn't shaved, his hair was unkempt, and at two thirty in the afternoon he was still wearing pyjama bottoms. What was worse, she thought she could also smell alcohol. She looked at his face more closely; his eyes were bloodshot.

"I have to get my shit together. Give me a few more days."

His speech was slurred. Helen followed behind as Linus walked slightly unsteadily back into the fug of the bedroom.

"This isn't going to help, all this drinking and smoking." Helen tried to keep the anger from her voice. "You need to sort yourself out! The police are scrutinising your computer trying to find God knows what, and no wonder Desi's dumped you if you've turned into a drunkard."

She was unprepared as he swung around wildly and grabbed her wrists.

"Yeah, I've fucked up pretty good! So just leave me alone!"

She struggled to free herself from the iron grip of his fingers.

"Let go! I've got to leave soon to get the children!"

She stumbled backwards as he relaxed his grasp and pushed her away.

"Piss off then! And don't send them up here!"

"No, I bloody well won't!" Helen regained her composure and stared at him. "You'll not be seeing any of us!"

He shrugged and turned away. Fighting back tears, Helen stormed out of the room and gave the door a satisfying slam before marching downstairs. She grabbed her bag and car keys, took a deep breath and walked towards the front door, closing it quietly behind her.

She felt a stab of envy; Emma with her highlighted blonde hair was quite the young lady now. Helen tried to smile as her 14 year old daughter, careful not to scuff her designer footwear, trod carefully down the somewhat grandiose staircase leading out into the school's front courtyard.

"Hi Mum! I'll sit in the car while you walk round and get the others. I've got a few texts to send."

"But you've only just said goodbye to your friends for the day!"

"I'm not texting *them.*" Emma rolled her eyes. "It's somebody else."

Helen sighed and wondered which 14 year old boy was trying to get into her daughter's knickers. She would have to try and gain access to the phone when Emma was asleep.

"I won't be long."

The preparatory annexe's playground was already heaving with mothers and children. Helen waved to Jack, loitering with friends by the main gate. Maria and Callum raced towards her.

"I won!" Callum poked his tongue out at Maria.

Maria pulled a face at her brother.

"'Cos you're bigger than me."

"Come on, let's go." Helen beckoned to Jack. "We've got somewhere else to go before we visit the park."

"Where?" Callum looked at her with interest.

"I've got to see Nanny first."

"Oh… I want to go to the *park.*" Maria complained.

"We will …afterwards." Helen beckoned to her son again. "*Jack!*"

The three younger children related aspects of their day as she drove along, but only Emma noticed her silence.

"Are you okay, Mum?"

Helen turned briefly towards her daughter sitting in the front seat.

"We're going to have to live with Nanny for a while. I just need to speak to her about it."

"Are you and Daddy getting a divorce?" Jack piped up from the back. "Oliver March's parents have split up too."

"Mind your own business!" Emma looked over her shoulder. "Mum hasn't said anything about a divorce."

Helen changed gear and managed a wry smile.

"No, we're not getting divorced. As you might have realised, things are a bit difficult between us at the moment, but as soon as Dad and I have sorted things out then we'll be able to move back home."

Maria wailed.

"I don't want to live with Nanny!"

"It's not *forever* …. Mum just *said*." Emma sighed at her sister. Suck it up!"

Helen clucked a 'tut' of annoyance.

"Don't use Americanisms."

"I'm not staying there, Mummy." Maria shook her head. "I want to come home with you and Daddy."

In a brief moment of silence while all four children digested the new information, Helen blocked out her last image of Linus and drove slowly along the gravel driveway of her mother's substantial home. As her offspring clambered out of the car, she saw the front door open.

"This is a surprise!" Ruth Hanson, 60 years old but very well preserved, smiled at Helen. "To what do I owe the pleasure?"

Helen closed the car doors and ushered her children inside.

"Need to speak to you, Mum. Can the kids have a swim?"

"Sure." Ruth nodded. "Their swimming costumes are still here from last time."

Helen felt careworn and old before her time as she watched her three youngest children frolicking about in the water and Emma, mobile phone in hand, stretching out languidly on a sun lounger. It was time to answer her mother's question.

"What's wrong, Helen?"

"Linus and I are having difficulties." Helen wiped away a tear. "I need to stay here for a while with the children."

She smiled at her mother, as Ruth laid a sympathetic hand over her own.

"I'll look after the children here, but you must go back to Linus and sort out your troubles. You won't achieve anything hiding away with me."

"I know." Helen sighed. "But …"

"*But* nothing." Ruth interrupted. "Go back home and don't worry about anything. The children will be fine with me. I'll take them to school, it's not far. I haven't got one foot in the grave just yet."

Helen laughed.

"I know you haven't! Thanks for this, yes I know I should be at home with Linus but it's somehow easier to stay here. I'll take Maria back with me though, as she'll make your life hell otherwise."

"Whatever you want, but don't take the easy option." Ruth waggled a finger. "Go home and sort your marriage out."

Helen nodded.

"Can I just stay here tonight? It'll give me more time to speak to the children about it all."

"Of course." Ruth replied. "Drop them in gently, and don't turn them against their father."

Helen dropped her thumb downwards.

"Too late for that, I'm afraid. Maria's the only one who doesn't believe me."

Chapter Twenty-Six

RICHARD JONES

The body had that bloated stomach-churning look of having been too long in the water. Richard covered his nose with his hand and mentally tried to compare the corpse's decayed features with the faxed photo of Steven Finch.

"We'll have to get dental records to identify him, even though he seems to be wearing the same shirt that's in the photo."

Luiz nodded.

"We need to be certain."

Richard, happy to let the forensic team carry on, walked up to his car through the gawping lovelies scattered along Leblon beach. Deaths were of course inevitable in his line of work, but the murderer had yet to be found and suddenly his own demise, whenever that might be, seemed far too close. Weighed down with the worries of the world, Richard tapped Tom Spicer's number into his phone. A sleepy voice yawned into his ear.

"Yeah?"

"Shit. Sorry Tom, I forgot … you're probably off duty now."

"I'm never off duty." Tom Spicer chuckled. "I was watching a film and dozed off, but hey, what's going on?"

"Looks like it might be Steven Finch's body laid out on Leblon beach. Forensics are going to check the dental records."

"I know what's coming." Tom sighed. "I'll get the job of telling his partner if it is."

Richard gave a wry chuckle.

"Sorry Mate, but I'm five and a half thousand miles away."

"Yeah, yeah." Tom replied drily. "Any bloody excuse…"

Richard gave a snort of pseudo-annoyance.

"Have you found anything on Ewing's computer?"

"Not yet." Tom exhaled with some force. "He's covered up his tracks pretty well, apart from an obvious affair with the Ingram woman. Keep hold of Martinez or Iglesias, whatever his name is, for a while longer."

"Will do. Keep looking, Tom. Something'll turn up."

Well past midnight, and the evening's festivities were still in full swing. Irritated at noise from the street and his inability to sleep, Richard climbed out of bed and put on a pair of shorts, trainers and a tee-shirt. He walked through the foyer of his hotel and out into the humid night air, deciding to take a circuitous route back passing heaving, noisy bars full of carefree twentysomethings unused to death and decay. Richard sighed and sweated as he walked, feeling old, cynical and care-worn.

On the spur of the moment he slipped into the nearest bar, with the faint hope that mingling with people thirty years' younger might magically lift his spirits. Music he did not recognise thumped into his ears, and the language was unfamiliar. Unlined faces stared his way in vague surprise. He pushed through the throng and elbowed a path to the counter.

"One beer, please."

The beer hardly touched the sides. Richard belched and held out his empty glass.

"Another."

Heat from the bodies all around him only made him sweat more, and overhead ceiling fans gave little relief. He squeezed one cheek of his backside onto a nearby stool and sipped his second pint more slowly, savouring the flavour and coolness of the brew.

He was aware that the well-dressed young man with long black hair slicked back into a ponytail had been watching him from a distance. Now he came in closer. Richard took another sip of beer and checked his watch.

"You're English, right?"

Richard shrugged.

"So?"

"So…" The young man replied with only a trace of an accent. "I have a message from Raul."

Richard stiffened on his stool, instantly alert.

"Out with it then. What is it?"

The young man wandered around to the back of the stool.

"This."

Richard felt a sharp pain in the middle of his back. He coughed and gasped for air.

"Sleep well, my friend."

The music's volume was suddenly not so troublesome on his eardrums. Concerned faces moved in and out of his consciousness, while his dying optic nerves sent out one last picture of the young man swiftly melting away into the crowd.

He felt slightly nervous addressing such a large congregation.

He looked around: uniformed officers sat side by side with family members. Tom took a deep breath and was encouraged by a weak smile from Sally Davidge, who sat dabbing her eyes in a wheelchair in the front row.

"I wanted to say a few words at Richard's service today. I had not known him long, but his motivation and determination to bring Jill Hayes' killer to justice should be an example to us all. Whether his death was a random assault or connected to his investigations, we may never know. There were no CCTV cameras in the bar and not one person present that night has come forward with any information, but even if the killer *had* been connected to the case and Richard *had* known in advance what was going to happen, I doubt he would have done anything differently."

A sniff emanated from somewhere in the middle of the church. Tom looked down briefly to check his notes, then carried on.

"Only God knows who killed Richard that night. God knows the secrets of all our hearts. Our investigations are ongoing, and new leads are coming in all the time."

He wondered whether God, if he existed, might be offended at the white lie. Tom turned over a leaf of his notebook and then turned his gaze towards the flower-bedecked coffin on its bier.

"Richard, thank you for the help you willingly offered me. If it takes me the rest of my life I will continue trying to discover why you died such a needless death."

Overcome with a sudden sadness, he stepped down from the dais and made his way back to an empty seat next to Sally, who leaned over and squeezed his hand.

"You did great, Tom."

The minister announced the next hymn and Tom stood back up while the organ pipes resonated around the church. However, he did not feel much like singing. Nor it appeared did the rest of the congregation, which caused the priest to raise his voice to counteract an obvious silence. Tom concentrated on Sally, staring down into her lap until the congregation were once again seated.

Finally it was with some relief that he stepped out of the cloying atmosphere of death into the churchyard and still strong autumn sunshine. With the tolling of the funeral bell in the background and Sally silently wheeling herself along beside him, he walked at the rear of the queue of mourners and clergy, and followed six undertakers carrying the coffin to its final newly-dug resting place in the family's plot. A younger version of Richard stepped forward to throw a handful of dirt onto the coffin as it was lowered into the ground on two wide straps. The vicar's sonorous tones rang out in the stillness:

"Forasmuch as it hath pleased Almighty God of his great mercy to take unto himself the soul of our dear brother here departed, we therefore commit his body to the ground; earth to earth, ashes to ashes, and dust to dust, in sure and certain hope of the resurrection to eternal life, through our Lord Jesus Christ."

Tom wondered why a god, any god, would have been pleased to receive the lifeless body of Richard Jones. He sighed as he bent down and picked up a fistful of earth. Sally, level with his ear, spoke quietly.

"What time is our flight back to Jersey?"

"Soon, I hope." Tom whispered. "I can't do any more for him here."

He waited his turn, let the earth fall onto Richard's coffin, and then pushed Sally back along a stony path towards their car. Her voice permeated his thoughts.

"Thank God it's over."

"Amen to that." He replied. "Let's get back to work."

He felt the landing gear descend and gazed out of the window as Jersey International Airport came into view. Sally tapped his arm.

"Penny for them?"

He rubbed his eyes and looked towards her.

"It bothers me that Luiz and his team might never find Richard's killer. Nobody saw anything, and even if they did, no-one's talking."

"Let's make sure Steven Finch's dental records match the body on the beach." Sally gathered her book and magazines together. "We'll take it one step at a time."

DESI INGRAM

She hated him now with a loathing that ate into her very core, and despised her momentary weakness at letting slip the love she had previously felt for him. Desi checked her bank balance again with undisguised dismay, and discovered with horror that she could now not afford to pay for her monthly highlights in Jersey's most exclusive salon. Visions of a cauliflower job at Maisie's *Cut Above* while Linus gloated in the background permeated many of her waking thoughts with a depressing frequency.

Dave's two bedroomed flat could hardly hold a candle to her previous abode, but at least she had finally been able to stop swatting him away like a fly after making it clear once and for all that she was not sixteen and silly anymore and desperate for sex. Desi tried to find a comfortable spot on the well-worn sofa, and wrinkled her nose while gazing at several unidentifiable stains on the carpet.

"Thanks for taking me in. When I've found a job I'll be out of here and you can have your flat back."

Dave shrugged.

"It's no trouble. Have you applied for any vacancies?"

"Yeah." Desi nodded. "But when they read my CV they say I'm over-qualified."

"Well, you were the head honcho at Starfaire with a six figure salary!"

His laugh irritated her beyond measure. Desi sighed.

"You work for that building company. Can you steal a piece of headed notepaper so I can type a fake CV? I'll give your number as my manager in case anyone phones to check."

"I'll try." Dave replied. "But it won't be easy."

"Nothing's easy in this world." Desi shook her head. "But I've just *got* to earn some money before I go bankrupt."

Desi sat up in bed with a start, heart pounding; she was even dreaming about him now. Through the thin walls of the flat Dave snored on, content with his lot. She climbed out of bed, padded along to the kitchen and flicked on the light, moving swiftly past the fat-splattered cooker towards the kettle.

There was half a pint of milk left in the fridge. Desi made a cup of comforting milky hot chocolate, and helped herself to the last three biscuits in the tin. She felt heavy and useless, and she knew her waist had expanded. She hated her impecuniousness, Dave's love of fast food, and his insistence on doing the weekly grocery shop. Money had always dripped through her fingers like water, but now it was not being replaced. She sipped froth off the top of the cup and considered ruefully that she had no idea at all of how to manage money.

By the time she had gulped the dregs, she knew what she had to do. She crept back to bed, but tossed and turned until she heard Dave go out to work at first light. After a shower, hair wash and several spoonfuls of sickly cereal she dressed in an Armani suit left over from her Starfaire days, but left the top button of the skirt undone and ensured a long satin blouse hid the result of too much fried food. At 9am she presented herself at the offices of the St. Helier Standard newspaper. She watched the over-made up receptionist eye the suit first and then herself.

"Can I help you?"

"I hope so." Desi gave her most dazzling smile. "I'd like to speak to one of your journalists, please."

The receptionist stood up.

"I'll check and see who's about for you."

She returned with a well-groomed forty-something man whom Desi might have flirted with in a past life, but now needed for quite a different purpose. She could hardly wait for her revenge.

"Good morning." The man held out his hand. "You'd like to speak to a journalist?"

Desi shook the warm, slightly soft hand.

"Yes please. In private if possible."

"Come this way. I'm Bob Jenkins." He lifted up the hinged counter. "I've an office at the back."

She liked the way his blond hair was clipped at the sides and back of his head, but left longer on the top. His shirt was crisp and freshly ironed (probably she thought by a loving wife), and a tight arse undulated slightly in designer jeans as he walked. Desi, hotter under the collar than she had felt for ages, mentally stamped on the butterflies in her stomach and sat down as indicated.

"What can I do for you?"

Desi had a good idea, but reluctantly decided to stick to the original plan.

"I'm Desi Ingram, who previously was in charge at Starfaire, the exam regulatory board."

Bob Jenkins looked across at her with undisguised interest.

"Oh yes?"

"Yes." Desi nodded. "I have information pertaining to the death of two people, and also to fraudulent practices at the Fideleter exam board, overseen by Mister Linus Ewing, MD of the publishing company Accelerat. I can give you this information according to how much you think it's worth. I have evidence via mobile phone texts. The police will need to be involved, as two murders have taken place, and I'll want immunity from prosecution for giving the information."

She enjoyed his rapt attention. Desi crossed one leg over the other and hoped the remaining buttons on her skirt stood up to the increased pressure and would not pop.

"Well, you've got me hooked already!" Bob held out a pen and notebook. "I'll have a word with my boss, and if you leave me your details I'll get back to you."

Desi, excitement mounting, scribbled down her name and phone number.

"Excellent! I'll arrange a meeting between us two and a member of the police force I know." Desi extended her hand. "I'll wait to hear from you."

Bob's hand, now somewhat clammy, shook hers.

"I'll get back later today, as it's not up to me to arrange payments."

"Fair enough." Desi smiled at him. "Let's hope your boss is feeling generous."

Chapter Twenty-Nine

SALLY DAVIDGE

She felt like a toddler taking its first steps. Sally grimaced at the physiotherapist as she gripped the railings with undisguised alarm.

"This is awful, Sue. I have to keep looking down to see where to put my leg."

Susan March smiled.

"Don't worry, you're doing fine. You'll soon get the hang of it and you'll be running around like a mountain goat, mark my words."

Sally began to sweat with the effort.

"I doubt that very much."

Her mobile phone rang as she returned to the relative safety of her wheelchair.

"Hello?

"Sally, it's Tom, can you talk?"

"Yeah, hang on."

His voice sounded upbeat. Sally, intrigued, wheeled herself back out to the empty waiting room.

"What's going on?"

"There's been a development in the Jill Hayes case."

"Spit it out then." Sally replied. "Don't keep it to yourself."

Tom chuckled.

"I'm meeting with Ms Ingram and a journalist later on today. It seems she has something to tell us."

"Ha!" Sally exhaled forcefully. "I'd come along too, but I'm supposed to be running Starfaire. I've given myself the morning off to attend physio, but I'd better be at work this afternoon just in case Linus Ewing pops in, although to be fair I haven't yet seen the guy."

"I'll keep you updated." Tom replied. "Over and out for now."

All the mail was now addressed to her alter ego, and as she opened the post Sally wondered whether Linus Ewing would ever manage to unearth Liz Trent's real identity. The lack of communication with Ewing unnerved her, and she wondered whether to turn up at the guy's house and announce herself; to her it seemed a good chance to check out how the land lay. The new leg was taking some getting used to, but at least now with the aid of a walking stick she could get herself in and out of her specially adapted car without needing any help.

Therefore it was with some slight trepidation that Sally pulled up outside the Ewing mansion after work and pressed an intercom attached to the gates, through which she could see two cars parked on the gravel drive next to the front porch.

"Hello? Can I help you?"

The female voice was well modulated and Sally had a mental impression of designer clothes, Roedean, Cheltenham Ladies College, lunch parties, big hats, gymkhanas and summer houses on the Italian Riviera.

"This is Liz Trent of Starfaire. I thought I'd come and introduce myself to Mr Ewing."

"Mr Ewing is not receiving visitors at the moment."

The tone was firm, but Sally was not to be deterred.

"When could I see him, then? I thought he'd like to meet the new girl who's taken over at Starfaire."

"He has your number. He'll call when he's free."

The intercom clicked off and the gates remained shut. Sally sat back down in the driver's seat and started up the engine, musing on her way home about the reason why Linus Ewing seemed not to want to be disturbed. When she pulled up on her driveway she was surprised to discover Fiona Cook sitting on a bench in the front garden. She stuck her head out of the driver's window and laughed.

"What are you doing here? It's not your cleaning day."

Fiona stood up.

"I fancied doing a bit of hoovering. Can I come in? I'm desperate for a wee."

"Of course!"

Sally walked slowly to the kitchen and took a surreptitious glance at Fiona from the doorway, as smartly dressed, the woman strode confidently back along the passageway from the bathroom.

"I must say, you really don't fit the usual image of a charwoman." Sally chuckled. "Want a cuppa before you start?"

"That'll be lovely." Fiona nodded. "And…actually… Tom sent me along to keep a watchful eye on you, although you're not supposed to know. I'm actually a DI, usually with Vice. I fancied a change to Homicide."

"I *knew* it!" Sally roared with laughter. "Please tell Tom I'm doing fine, especially now I've got my leg back."

"Things might get a bit sticky now Desi Ingram has had a word with Tom." Fiona sat down at the kitchen table. "I've been assigned to your spare room, in fact."

Sally, intrigued, left the kettle untouched and sat down opposite Fiona.

"What's happened?"

"Plenty." Fiona sighed. "Tom wanted me to let you know he has a warrant and that he and the team will be making an early morning visit to arrest Ewing tomorrow. Ms Ingram has shown mobile phone messages from Linus Ewing pertaining to Jill Hayes' death from a pay-as-you-go phone he gave her. Jill was making too many enquiries about their little money making exam caper. It appears that one of the Starfaire staff, Steven Finch, was paid two hundred and fifty thousand pounds to carry out the murder. From other messages it's clear Finch then scarpered to Rio, but washed up on Leblon beach, as you know. According to Ms Ingram, Linus Ewing paid Carlos Iglesias to ensure Finch's silence."

"And what about Richard?" Sally pictured her former colleague in her mind's eye."

"He was getting too close to the truth as well, we believe." Fiona sat forward in her chair. "Carlos Iglesias is on the Accelerat payroll as a sleeping, perhaps even invisible, partner. He'll be charged back in Rio with organising Steven and Richard's murders. Desi Ingram kept all the messages as a form of insurance, just in case anything went wrong, I suppose."

"And it has by the sound of it." Sally replied. "But why would she shop Ewing now?"

"Don't know." Fiona shrugged. "Something's gone on and she's not saying, but all we do know is that she's singing like a bird in return for immunity from prosecution. It seems our friend Ewing knows people who move on the dark side of life, and he'll use them to make sure he gets what he wants."

Sally stood up and grabbed her stick.

"This definitely calls for a cup of tea." She smiled at Fiona. "Sugar?"

There was nothing to get up for. Linus lay supine in pyjama bottoms on top of the duvet and blew a perfect smoke ring towards the ceiling. Below he could hear Helen's muffled voice talking on the intercom. He looked at his watch; *who the fuck wanted to speak to his wife at six thirty in the morning?*

Intrigued, he rolled off the bed, crept towards the door and opened it a few inches. *Was there a new man?*

The long 'ping' as Helen activated the outside gate from the intercom intrigued him. He padded out onto the landing and bent over the balcony.

"Who's coming in?"

Helen appeared at the foot of the stairs and glared up at him.

"Tom Spicer and three other policemen. I'd get dressed if I were you."

A wave of panic washed over him. Linus ran into the bedroom and locked the door. With insides churning, he had a quick wash at the small en-suite sink and grabbed the first pair of boxer shorts, jeans and tee-shirt that he could see in his wardrobe. He threw on a pair of socks and trainers, and reluctantly opened the bedroom door when he heard Spicer's voice on the other side. Four burly men in uniform stood next to Helen and blocked his exit.

"Linus Ewing, I have a warrant for your arrest in connection with the deaths of Jill Hayes, Steven Finch, and DI Richard Jones. You have a right to remain silent, but anything you *do* say may be used as evidence against you in a court of law."

Linus shrugged, stood his ground, and willed his heart to regain its regular beat.

"You're mistaken, Spicer. I have no idea what you're talking about."

"Save it." Tom Spicer produced a pair of handcuffs. "Ms Ingram has told us all we need to know."

Linus felt nauseous as the handcuff bit into his wrist, even though his stomach was empty. He blurted a response with the last of his bravado.

"Whatever she's told you, it's a lie! She's pissed off because I sacked her. I want to speak to my lawyer."

"Of course." Spicer applied the other handcuff to his wrist. "You can make a phone call when we're back at the station."

To Linus's horror, a small figure appeared on the top floor landing and wailed.

"Daddy. What's happening?"

Maria, clad in her nightshirt, ran downstairs towards him but was intercepted by Helen, who picked up her daughter.

"Daddy has to go with these officers for now. Now you know why I wanted you to stay with Nanny like your brothers and sister."

"I'll be back soon, darling." Linus felt a tugging as Spicer began to move towards the stairs. "Don't worry."

With the shame of his wife and child looking on, Linus felt himself ushered at speed towards the main door and then out to where a police Range Rover had parked on the front gravel. With two officers either side of him on the back seat, there was no escape. Linus, head down and eyes closed, silently stabbed a mental effigy of Desi Ingram.

Helen buried her face in her daughter's warm neck, and shivered with trepidation at the knowledge that she was now a single parent. She realised with alarm that she had always depended on Linus more than she should have. Now it was time to face reality and be strong for the sake of her children.

Two days' later Desi, ninety thousand pounds richer, poured a second cup of coffee into one of Dave's grimy cups and gazed with a gloating contentment upon Bob Jenkins' article on the front page of the St. Helier Standard. Linus' downfall had been complete, with an upcoming court hearing in which she had agreed to testify. All the dirty linen had been washed in plain view, and the public were eating up the disclosures. Fideliter would never again serve exam papers, and after the takeover of Starfaire there would be new personnel not connected with the now defunct Accelerat. She might have felt sorry for Liz Trent had she been a genuine employee, but inside Desi still smarted with the knowledge that she had been duped by a charming one legged policewoman.

She sipped the scalding liquid, revolted by the smell of Dave frying bacon and eggs a few feet away. He turned a hairless chest towards her, removed the saucepan with its sizzling contents from the heat, and waved a spatula in the air.

"Bacon sarnie?"

She suddenly felt thoroughly nauseated. Her breasts ached, and her waist was not reducing despite a week of eating next to nothing. *And where the hell was her period?* Desi, gripped with a growing and unwelcome realisation, stood up and just about made it to the toilet. As she retched into the bowl, she heard Dave come into the bathroom and felt him hold her hair away from her face.

"Are you okay, Des?"

"Do I look like I'm okay?" Desi coughed and retched. "I think I might be bloody pregnant!"

"Christ!" Dave stepped back. "You've *got* to be joking!"

Stomach contents expelled and feeling weak, Desi stood up slowly from her crouched position.

"It's no joke. I *feel* different. Oh fuck… *I haven't had a period for three months!"*

She had always been in tight control of her life, her lovers, and her employees. With an increasing panic threatening to consume her, she imagined sleepless nights with a bawling incontinent infant, the father of which at this precise moment was sadly indeterminate. Desi, wretched, rinsed her mouth and stared at Dave's reflection in the mirror.

"I'll go to the supermarket and get one of those ClearBlue things. I need to know for sure."

"It can't be mine." Dave shook his head. "We only did it a couple of times, and anyway, I used a *Johnny* like you asked."

Desi sighed.

"I never had any scares with condoms before, but then I read graffiti on a Durex machine. Some bright spark had written '*My dad says these don't work.*"

"Nah, nah, you're not blaming this one on me. It's *his*… it's Ewing's fucking kid. You'll have to get *him* to pay."

Shards of hot, white anger coursed through her veins.

"I'll ask all the prospective fathers to take a paternity test! Does that suit you? Just get out and leave me alone!"

She slammed the door at his retreating back, and then sat down on the toilet seat and sobbed. Life was not panning out quite how she had envisaged.

Dan Hayes batted a tennis ball towards where Jordan stood eyeing up two teenage girls walking past.

"Keep your mind on the game!"

The ball whizzed back at him with attitude.

"Will do, Dad!"

Dan laughed as he remembered his own angst-filled adolescence. He was relieved to see that Jordan was slowly recovering from his mother's death. Sure, there were times when the boy would seek him out and howl into his shoulder, but those times had become less frequent now. They had forged a bond together in their grief. What was more, Dan had definitely taken a liking to Sally, who had always kept him in the loop with any developments in the case. He had been quite surprised to discover her real vocation, and had felt a strange sadness when he heard that she had been posted to St. Helier. However, during her last phone call to him she had let slip that now her friend's murderer had been brought to justice, she would soon be winging her way back to the mainland. Dan thudded the ball back to Jordan with a gleam in his eye that had not been there for some time.

Sue Young stuffed the last of the old Fideliter Health & Carer scripts into an envelope and mused on how Jill Hayes had been correct all along; the questions *were* too easy for students on the verge of adulthood. She felt a pang of regret for the way she had treated her erstwhile colleague, but to have spoken out against Fideliter and consequently suffered the combined forces of Linus Ewing and Desi Ingram's rage, even from their convenient hidey-hole on Jersey, would have probably meant having to find a new job.

At nearly 50 years of age Sue knew her chances of securing alternative employment were now relatively slim. She would miss the annual 'bonus' paid into her offshore bank account, but she knew that sooner or later all good things usually come to a natural end. She had made a sizeable profit through shrewd investments, and with any luck her old age would be spent in relative comfort. Sue mused on the fact that if only Jill Hayes'd had the sense to keep her mouth shut, she too would have eventually been the proud owner of a magically self-filling Jersey bank account.

As a result of the revelations the entire nation had discovered through watching the latest BBC News bulletins, Sue looked forward to the fresh wind of change that would presently be blowing through Daxton College. Without warning John Bream and several inspectors had tendered their resignations, and interviews for new staff would soon be taking place.

Sue sat back in her chair and sighed. *Were there actually any genuine colleges left who did not fiddle exam papers or exam results to make themselves look good in league tables? And how much had Ewing paid Bream to ensure his silence?* Now that Fideliter had been wound up and presumably subsequent Health & Carer exam pass rates might therefore fall, she wondered just how long it would be before students 'discovered' the answers to their exam questions before they had even sat the tests.

She shook her head, wrote an address on the envelope, and put it in the outgoing post for marking.

Chapter Thirty-One

THREE YEARS LATER

Helen peeped out through a glass panel in the front door as she pressed a button to open the security gate, but hardly recognised the once-svelte figure pushing a pram along the gravel. Desi Ingram had gained roughly two stones in weight, and her hair hung lank upon her shoulders. An overweight toddler strapped into the pram screamed loudly at his enforced incarceration, and thrashed his arms and legs about in a vain effort to break free. Helen opened the door and prepared to greet her ex-husband's erstwhile lover.

"Desi. To what do I owe the pleasure?"

She hoped the woman picked up on her sarcasm. The boy screamed louder. Desi took out a packet of crisps from her bag and shoved them into the toddler's hand. In the ensuing quietness, Desi pushed the pram to one side.

"I wanted to come here today, because I finally got Dave to take a paternity test. As you know, Linus wouldn't."

"Oh?" Helen looked at the boy stuffing his face, and could see no resemblance to any of her children."

"Yeah. Oscar is Dave's kid. I thought I'd do my good deed for the day and let you know."

"Well, it's got nothing to do with me now." Helen shrugged. "But thanks anyway."

Desi nodded.

"You're welcome. How's Linus doing?"

"As you know, we're now divorced." Helen shrugged. "I only visit him because Maria wants to go. It's a bit like the *Shawshank Redemption* in there. Linus gives advice to all the inmates about keeping hold of their ill-gotten gains. I'd like to tell them never to believe a word he says, but he seems to have created quite a fan base in there."

"Sounds like Linus." Desi chuckled. "Dave and I still live together. I've not managed to find work yet, what with having to look after Oscar, but Dave's finally coming around to the thought of being a father. He's even taken Oscar to the park a couple of times now."

Helen wondered when Desi was going to leave.

"Glad to hear it. Thanks for coming by."

She moved nearer the door as Desi swung the pushchair around.

"I loved him; you know." Desi smiled at Helen. "But he loved you more. I'm sure of it. He would never have left you had you not divorced him."

Helen stepped back onto the inner welcome mat.

"It's all water under the bridge now. When Linus eventually gets out he'll still have to keep in touch with me because of

Maria, but that's as far as it goes and he'll be free to see anybody he wants to. It was hard at first, but I'm doing okay on my own. You're welcome to him."

"Cheers for the tip." Desi laughed and walked away. "We'll see what the future holds."

THE END.

Before You Go…

If you have enjoyed this novella, you may also like ***'Cruising Danger'***, also by Stevie Turner.

https://books2read.com/u/4DE5DQ

Blurb

When Pauline Edmunds agrees to accompany her workmate Shirley on a Caribbean cruise, she is disappointed to be left alone almost at the start when Shirley starts a holiday romance with Joe Collins, a guitarist in a band working on board the ship. However, Pauline does not like the look of Joe, and tries to dissuade Shirley from continuing the affair. When Shirley cannot be found one morning, Pauline begins to investigate her friend's disappearance, opening up a whole can of worms amidst a background of Caribbean scenery and sunshine.

Other Books by Stevie Turner

THE PILATES CLASS
A HOUSE WITHOUT WINDOWS
FOR THE SAKE OF A CHILD
LILY: A SHORT STORY
NO SEX PLEASE, I'M MENOPAUSAL!
A RATHER UNUSUAL ROMANCE
THE DAUGHTER-IN-LAW SYNDROME
REVENGE
THE NOISE EFFECT
CRUISING DANGER
THE DONOR
REPENT AT LEISURE
LIFE: 18 SHORT STORIES
ALYS IN HUNGERLAND
MIND GAMES
LEG-LESS AND CHALAZA
PARTNERS IN TIME
FINDING DAVID: A PARANORMAL SHORT STORY

About The Author

Stevie Turner writes suspense, women's fiction, and darkly humorous novels. She won a New Apple Book Award in 2014 and a Readers' Favorite Gold Award in 2015 for 'A House Without Windows', and one of her short stories, 'Checking Out', was published in the Creative Writing Institute's 2016 anthology 'Explain!' Her psychological thriller 'Repent at Leisure' won third place in the 2016 Drunken Druid Book Award contest.

Stevie lives in East Anglia, UK, and is married with two sons and four grandchildren. She has also branched out into the world of audio books, screenplays, and translations. Most of her novels are now available as audio books, and one screenplay, 'For the Sake of a Child', won a silver award in the Spring 2017 Depth of Field International Film Festival. 'A House Without Windows' gained the attention of a New York media production company in December 2017. Some of Stevie's books have been translated into German, Spanish, and Italian.

Social Links

Website:
http://www.stevie-turner-author.co.uk/

Twitter:

http://www.twitter.com/StevieTurner6

Goodreads:

https://www.goodreads.com/author/show/7172051.Stevie_Turner

Printed by Amazon Italia Logistica S.r.l.
Torrazza Piemonte (TO), Italy